Jacky West

D1796187

The
Real
Big
BANG

An environmentally friendly book printed and bound in England by
www.printondemand-worldwide.com

Mixed Sources
Product group from well-managed
forests, and other controlled sources
www.fsc.org Cert no. TT-COC-002641
© 1996 Forest Stewardship Council
FSC

PEFC Certified
This product is
from sustainably
managed forests
and controlled
sources
PEFC
www.pefc.org
PEFC/16-33-415

This book is made entirely of chain-of-custody materials

www.fast-print.net/store.php

THE REAL BIG BANG
Copyright © Jacky West 2014

Illustrated by Jacky West
Edited by Maria Jackson

All rights reserved

No part of this book may be reproduced in any form by photocopying
or any electronic or mechanical means, including information storage
or retrieval systems, without permission in writing from both the
copyright owner and the publisher of the book.

All characters are fictional.
Any similarity to any actual person is purely coincidental.

The right of Jacky West to be identified as the author of this work has
been asserted by her in accordance with the Copyright, Designs and
Patents Act 1988 and any subsequent amendments thereto.

A catalogue record for this book is available from the British Library

ISBN 978-178456-067-6

First published 2014 by
FASTPRINT PUBLISHING
Peterborough, England.

For Meo, ever enthusiastic and helpful,
Robbo, the clown, always in the thick of it and Ezay
Dollar, who took us back to the future.

Chapter 1

No one knew how Red Kep became the centre of the space race
or how the locals came across the technology in the first place.
The whole shebang was mind-boggling to the point of sci-fi,
but somehow they did and so must take their place in history as
such. Anyway, all stories should start at the beginning; so
we'll return to those far off heady days of the fifties when the
radio (for the television was still in its infancy and only for the
rich) flooded and saturated everybody with tales of two-headed,
ten-eyed, green-backed, claw-footed, dog-breathed monsters
from space or just Martians from Mars. Mars wasn't so far
away. After all, as far as space goes, it was in our solar system
and kind of down the street a little. So with the power of radio,
and the greater power of people's imaginations, fuelled by
comic books and authors such as Ray Bradbury and H. G.
Wells, to name but a few, it was to be a ripe old time for space
mongering.

Sleepy, maybe even dozy, little Red Kep sat in the flat fenlands
of East Anglia. It took its name from the big red hill that
overlooked the town; the only feature on a green, fertile
landscape. Mr Knowles, historian and village teacher and less
kindly known as Mr Know-It-All by everyone who knew him,

explained to those who would listen that the name originated from northern European settlers to the area many moons before. As he was nearly always right in such matters no one questioned him.

Red Kep existed in post-war Britain as a market gardening and farming community growing foodstuffs for an expanding population. So the people of Red Kep were in the business of feeding a nation. One such feeder was Mr Alec Green. You know how in a group of dogs there will always be one trying to be the leader? He'll snap at the other dogs, terrorise them, cajole, demoralise and bully the others at every opportunity until, finally, they accept him as boss. You see it many times in different walks of life, in the playground, at work, within the family. There is always competition, always one trying to be top, hence the saying 'Top Dog.'

So Alec Green thought of himself as being top of the tree. Green's claim to fame, (or so he thought), was his vegetables or to be exact his brussels sprouts. Everyone at some time or other has eaten those horrible, old, green, mushy, pongy things that we all love to push to the sides of our plates only to be met with cries from adults of, 'If you don't eat your greens, you won't grow up to be big and strong.' Eventually children usually give in with yelps of 'ughhh!' as they go through the hideous, mind-bending ritual once again. Trying not to taste, moving the greens around their mouths without biting, some are even taken to holding their noses as they swallow the rotting vegetation in the hope they will disappear once and for all. Greens! Uggghhh! It was like something you avoided on the pavement. You know.......squishy, horrible, repugnant. Now if they were covered in ice cream....mmmm that would be different.

Alec Green, green by name, green by nature, was one such pushy parent. His other half, Gwen was a frail looking woman. Her hair was usually covered in straw while her wellies gave off the fragrance of eau de compost. She was more scarecrow than woman, a sad belittled weed who withered in the shadow of her overpowering husband. Where he ploughed she followed. Never questioning, she played the role of the humble servant. Just the way Alec Green liked it, for after all he had his plants to talk to and didn't need any interference from any human involvement.

'Keep shovelling that manure dear. Those veggies are growing as we speak. Loverly,' were some of Green's words of encouragement to his wife. The only problem was that he did the talking and Mrs Green had to do the listening, always the listening! Green was one of those people who didn't value anyone else's opinion and in conversation smothered out any resistance or challenge until it was only himself talking. We've all met his type at sometime. You're ten minutes into a discussion and the only words you are uttering are '......ah.......nnnn....yes....so...' And at the end of it they usually say something like, 'I see you have the same views as myself. Great!'

Even though at the end of this 'conversation' you feel like screaming, 'I haven't said a word you flaming moron. I have more in common with a skunk with a severe case of gastric enteritis after eating a sixteen-week-old vindaloo curry. In other words I have nothing at all in common with you but speaking of skunks.' Though you think all of this, you are too nice a person to say any of it. The other person has run their mouth off and you have been bullied into a submissive position, but do you care. No. You, will in future, avoid this person as you would that skunk with his gippy tummy. So it was with Mrs Green. She sought only to humor her husband when the need arose, no more, no less.

Their offspring, the result of cross-pollination of the human species, as Alec Green called it, consisted of two children. They were named Peter and Primrose and were aged ten and eight respectively. Peter was named after an uncle on his father's side and Primrose named after a wild flower. She was very lucky not to be named Begonia but as her mother had kept up the pretence of mispronouncing the word, as Beg yin a, Alec Green fell victim to the ploy. The flowery element remained to become Primrose. Begonia was buried in the compost heap forever. Mrs Green's first small, subtle victory over the green monster. She breathed a sigh of relief that the child wouldn't be handicapped by such a name as Begonia and was glad that her husband didn't come up with Daffodil. Imagine, she thought, being called Daffy for short. She shuddered at the very mention of the flower. Though the connection with the Green family and horticulture wasn't to end there.

'A chip off the old potato,' said Alec Green referring to his son. And wasn't he just. Peter was sprouting up like a shot spud that's been in the dark too long as it searches for a touch of sunlight. With blonde hair, blue eyes and a pair of cheeks that looked like he had swallowed two footballs, (the result of eating too many hard apples), Peter looked pretty normal. Well ……..nearly. His sister was the small, pretty, flowers-in-the-hair type of child who loved the outdoors. So the two of them were sort of normal as children go, but they became kind of strange when you looked at them a little closer. In this case

Green was their surname and green was their color.

'Aaaagghhh!' shrieked many a child on first setting eyes on one of the Green siblings only to be told by a nervous parent, 'Now it's bad manners to stare.'

Stare! Stare…how could you not when someone………..when someone was…well, green! Though we all know there is more than one shade of Green. Forty we are told, so this being the case we can class the Green children as emerald and a nice translucent one at that. Anyhow, speaking of differences, let's move onto the start of the new school term and the emergence of a new face in Red Kep.

Miss Sally waited in anticipation as she greeted the children in her new class. This was Miss Jemima Sally's first job after teacher training and though she did not particularly want to go into teaching, she now saw the opportunity to help others and fully intended to give this teaching malarkey her best shot.

'Hullo,' she said to some of the children while a smile served a better purpose for some of the more timid types.

'Hullo, Miss,' was the reply she often heard back as the returning children did not know the new Miss's surname. It was to be one of the first items on Miss Sally's agenda, when she got them all settled of course. She was immediately aware of differences in all of the children. Some, rather all, were there because they had to be but she could tell, feel, that some of the children found the school environment alien. Others thought that it was just another place to mix with their friends. Miss Sally felt better knowing that she was going to be in charge of the Primary Four pupils who tended to be less of a handful than the more boisterous early year students.

The children were of a mixed bunch, some were from the nearby airbase and the remainder from the village farming community. As was the case with the start of most school years some children returned quite happily, while others had an 'I wish I were somewhere else' attitude. Miss Sally hoped to have them all eager little school lovers in the first few hours. It was then that Miss Sally spied Primrose Green.

Not that it was hard to find Primrose among a group of others. She was wearing only the skimpiest faded blue dress with a pair of leather sandals. Not even the color of her effulgent emerald green face, the result of too much chlorophyll, from which peered a pair of unusual violet eyes and below her blood red lips…. This all seemed normal enough. Well, sort of. It was what sat on top of her head that drew the most attention. What should have been a mop of straw colored hair was in fact, from Miss Sally's point of view ….'Aaaaghhh!'

'Is that an equatorial rain forest you've got on your head, girl,' Miss Sally felt like screaming.

'Or would you like me to cut a few of those trees out of the way with this chainsaw, just in case your eco-system is a little unbalanced.'

Though she felt like saying something along those lines, Miss Sally, being the nice person that she was, looked calmly at Primrose Green and smiled. Primrose responded with a flash of her eyes before finding a seat in the classroom.

To be fair it wasn't that Primrose's coiffure was bad. It was more like an unkempt garden that needed a bit of pruning here and there, starting with the array of wild flowers. Here was a flower child long before flower children were even thought of. Neglect was a word that sprung straight to Miss Sally's mind. She wondered what sort of country they lived in where you needed a licence for a dog but not so much as a used dog-eared return train ticket to Brighton to be in charge of the future health of a young body and mind. In fact animals, if need be, could revert to fending for themselves but children were an entirely different matter. What would she, Miss Sally, have turned into if she had been left to her own devices? Miss Sally smiled to herself. Probably a lot happier than she was at that particular moment. She sighed for at least they were all seated. Time for roll call.

Miss Sally cleared her throat readying herself to use her most authoritarian voice, as her real tone was usually very faint and shrill. 'Good morning children,' she began.

'Good morning, Miss,' came back the reply from the class.

'My name is Miss Sally,' she said, continuing as her voice started to slip back into its normal faintness.

'And I think we shall start with the roll call.'

Finishing, Miss Sally slipped on her spectacles then started to scan the register on her desk.

'Andrew Archibald,' she called out, reading from the first name on the register.

'Here, Miss,' came the reply from the immaculately dressed, pressed and starched, cardboard cut-out seated in the classroom front row. It seemed to Miss Sally's eyes at least to be a cardboard cut-out. So stiff was the boy sitting that she feared at any moment a breeze might break him in half. She marked Archibald down as one of the air force children. There were a few around and Miss Sally imagined his father to be a drill sergeant who ironed and starched the boy in the evening, before popping him under his mattress to be rolled out again in the morning.

'Hup, two, hup, two, hup, two. Off you go to school, lovely boy. Hup.... Hup.'

'Hhhhmmm,' mused Miss Sally as she moved on to the next name on the register.

'Samantha Bradley?'

'Here,' yawwwwnnneed Samantha Bradley. 'Miss.' she finished clamping a hand over her mouth to stifle another yawn.

'Just how I feel myself,' thought Miss Sally. She eyed the dark-haired, ringleted girl with cheeks the color of red apples and gave a yawn herself before continuing with the register.

'Francesca Dewhurst,' said Miss Sally.

'Yes,' was the reply from the rear of the class.

Miss Sally still had to put a face to the name but made a tick beside the register anyway. She was starting to tire of the formal pronunciation of everyone's name. Francesca Dewhurst was in reality, probably, better known as Franny to her family and friends instead of the pompous and rather snobby sounding Francesca. Not that the girl was anything like that in reality. Shudder the thought. It was just the case that names tended to give a first, sometimes false, impression. Or so Miss Sally thought.

'Bert!' started Miss Sally, letting her attention lapse for a second before continuing as if nothing had happened.

'Robert Eccles?' Without looking up from the page and going with her first impression of the name Miss Sally envisaged a Bert Eccles to be of farming stock, squat build, and curly hair with a ruddy outdoor complexion.

'Here, Miss,' came back the reply from the young Eccles, drawing Miss Sally's attention to compare the real picture with her imaginative portrait.

She spied the long, stringy necked, straight, dark-haired chap as he towered nearly a head above all the other children even when seated. She was completely and utterly wrong in her view of how Bert Eccles should have looked. With a name as British as bangers and mash, the real Bert Eccles looked more like an Antonio or a Sebastian. Definitely some foreign blood in his genes, more pasta than mashed potato. False impressions once again, though she thought she may have been right about the farming part. She sighed as she tired of the game.

'Primrose Green?' she muttered to herself as she read the name from the register. Miss Sally looked around the classroom. 'Primrose Green,' she said aloud. She met with no reaction as a host of little faces stared back in her direction.

'Primrose Green?' said Miss Sally once more, though louder this time.

She caught the movement of the class as the children shuffled, turned and squirmed to look for Primrose Green. There was silence as everyone's eyes fell on Primrose Green. How Miss Sally had missed the girl seated in the back row was beyond her, though she thought the reason was that she had mistaken her for a potted plant. Primrose was oblivious to all around her as she doodled away on a scrap of paper. 'Take that dandelion stem out of your ears!' Miss Sally felt like screaming, but being Miss Sally, she didn't. At that moment Primrose's seated neighbour gave the girl a nudge, causing her to glance up to face the reception of staring peepers that looked in her direction.

'Primrose Green?' repeated Miss Sally once again, though quieter this time, as she knew she had the girl's attention.

'Ah. Here Miss,' said Primrose. She felt her cheeks start to flush with embarrassment, which only caused her to turn a darker shade of green.

'Oh crikey! She's turning into a Martian slime ball!' said a boy's voice, which some of the class responded to by giggling. Feeling the tension mounting and the ever growing darkening green fire in Primrose Green's cheeks, Miss Sally lifted a heavy book above her head and flung it unto her desktop. The situation was averted in a split second as all eyes shifted away from Primrose to the noise, then the stern looking face of Miss Sally.

'If I should hear another squeak out of turn there will be a session of detention after class.' said Miss Sally putting on her most fearsome deep voice only reserved for the most dire of situations.

'Do I make myself clear? Do I?'

'Yes, Miss,' was the reply as one from the children.

Miss Sally glanced over her glasses pleased that the color had drained back into Primrose's face to something close to normality. If Miss Sally was looking for names or descriptions to match people's mannerisms she need look no further. Primrose Green was a definitive case. Miss Sally fancied the local health visitor nurse would have a field day, literally, considering there was one on top of the girl's head, when it came to giving Primrose the once over.

Everyone who has ever been to school remembers the yearly health visitor who comes to check their welfare. We've all experienced the eye tests, hearing tests, quick look down the old gullet and finally a prod round the thatch as they look for bugs, nits or whatever they call them. You know those creepy, crawly things that can be passed on by your best friends at school. So, if you happen to have any, you are duly congratulated by the health visitor, given a sticky lolly to rot what remains of your teeth, then told it's all very fine and nits only live in clean hair anyway. So there you are a big smile on your face, your own little world living atop your cranium and then you're told to use some extra special shampoo on your little friends. Little wonder you are confused, when you come away from the nurse and start telling everyone how special you are and asking if they would like a peak at your pet colony, only to find that everyone runs in the other direction, screaming,

'Unclean! Unclean!' Adults lying once again thought Miss Sally. Not that she thought Primrose would be harbouring any bugs. She imagined the health visitor was more likely to encounter a tiger, a ferocious nurse-eating tiger at that. How she hated being lied to when she was a child. Grownups, bah! Miss Sally bit her bottom lip subconsciously, which brought her out from her daydream back to the roll call. In a few hurried seconds she rushed through the remainder of the names.

As it was the start of a new school year, Miss Sally decided she would have to assess how for her pupils had progressed in their previous year. Pushing back her glasses onto her fine nose Miss Sally mused over where she would start; arithmetic, writing or reading? The good old Three Rs. Arithmetic might be a bit much, especially as it was their first day back and most pupils, or so she thought, found it one of the most boring subjects. Well, if she was honest, she hadn't really liked it herself at their age, so why should she lumber them with something she loathed when there were better things to do.

She got up from her desk and stood next to the window, which overlooked the school grounds. The movement of getting up from her chair caused her glasses to slide down her nose again. She really would have to get a pair that fitted, she reminded herself. They were always doing that. It was just at that moment, for Jemima Sally was short-sighted, that she glanced out of the second storey window.

'Shake my old granny's rocking chair!' she said, her eyes nearly popping out of her head as she re-adjusted her glasses, 'I really must get a new pair of gleeks.'

For a moment, for a fraction of a second, Miss Sally thought she had seen a boy in mid-scream, his tonsils dangling at the back of a huge dark cavern which was the beginning of his throat, as he sought to gasp air in the new environment he found himself in---------that of the birds. To all intents and purposes the scream was silent; as she was sure it would be if you were launched into space without a second's notice and no wings with which to fly. Miss Sally couldn't make up her mind what she saw, though she knew she had spent most of the morning daydreaming. She made another mental note to get her eyesight looked at as soon as possible. What would she be seeing next? Pink elephants or worse? She turned back to her pupils.

Chapter 2

Rev. Jasper pushed his bicycle along Red Kep's high street. It was not so much the high street as the only street in the village. Jasper, grey haired and going thin on top, was starting to put on a few pounds of extra blubber as he neared his fiftieth year. He found it easier to get around the village on his bicycle instead of walking. For this reason, as well as his ever expanding waistline, was known affectionately, though not so secretly, by the locals as the Biking Jelly Belly or B.J.B. for short. Every now and then Jasper would hear his nickname as he came upon a few unsuspecting members of his flock. He revelled in their discomfort as he inquired, 'Talking about me are you?' He would be met generally with protestations from the participants that they were discussing something entirely unrelated, but, being a man who could take a joke, he was quick to put them at ease with a few kindly words.

So Rev. Jasper found himself outside Kale Knarsnock's printing shop. Knarsnock was a rare name for any east country villager but anyone could tell from his accent that the printer was from far-off shores. Rumour circulated that Knarsnock was of Norwegian lineage arriving at Red Kep as a survivor from a merchant marine vessel that fell victim to a torpedo off the east coast during the war. Eventually he settled in Red Kep using his quite considerable skills of printing to keep the villagers amused with a weekly rag on local news and throwing together an array of any other literature, signs, posters, cards or the like that they required. How a merchant seaman was proficient in the art of printing nobody thought to ask.

A small, bearded, ferret-faced character with red colored hair he was as thin as a racing snake. Though he had an average command of English, which led to some very amusing and embarrassing moments in the past, he was always willing to spend a few moments having a chinwag. A bit of an old gossip would be the best way to describe Knarsnock, he was always in the thick of it, pulling any story he could from left, right or centre. He was the complete chronicler of events around Red Kep. Knarsnock was the helm of the Red Kep Recorder and though he took in items from other writers, he tried to be printer, editor and journalist all rolled into one. This brought him a lot of publicity, not so much for his literary talent but more for his bloomers, (and not the kind you wear).

Rev. Jasper propped his bike up outside the shop then entered through the faded red painted door. A bell clattered away in some far away part of the shop as Jasper let the door swing shut. It was like entering another world as the dark dusty semi-lit interior enveloped Rev. Jasper. Jasper blinked as his eyes adjusted to the dinginess. He heard the scurrying before he identified the figure of Knarsnock leering out from the darkness. His green cat-like eyes peered over the top of his dust covered counter, as he gave a small smile to expose yellow fang like teeth. Rev. Jasper sniffed the air around Knarsnock which smelled of earth. Perhaps he had been doing some gardening. 'Are you today, how? Rev. Jasper,' said Knarsnock in his very thick hard to detect accent.

As was his way he always misplaced the odd word. People around Red Kep reckoned the reason for this was Knarsnock thought in Norwegian and then had to translate into English. Of course the English language is hard for the English to understand, never mind a Norwegian seaman.

Jasper nodded his head then said, 'Fine, fine. Busy though. You know how it is, with the church and all the business with the flower and veg show coming up.'

Knarsnock wrinkled his nose causing his moustache to move as a mouse would move his whiskers.

'Coming za flower show! Yes?' Knarsnock said, exposing more of his yellowed fangs. 'That's what I've just said,' thought Jasper but not in so many words. 'Strange little fellow.'

'Yes the flower show. That time of the year again I'm afraid,' said Jasper aloud. 'Have you got the thingy-ma-jiggy ready?' The Reverend was always forgetting words but always interloped with another interpretation. His sentences were always littered with thingy-ma-jigs, something-or-others or his favourite, 'you-know-what-I-mean.'

Well if someone happened to know what he meant, then that person would be nothing short of a mind reader, so the Reverend wouldn't have to open his thingy-ma-jiggy mouth in the first place. The Reverend's absent mindedness could be very infuriating at times to others. Now Knarsnock was on the receiving end.

'Ma-jiggy-thingies. Dat wots den?' said the man-ferret back-to-front and meaning though not saying. 'What's that then?'

'Oh, the something-or-other leaflets,' said the Rev. pausing for a second.

'Oh, you know for the flower show,' he finished letting out a laugh.

'Ah ha! You mean da posters,' said Knarsnock.

Jasper clapped his hands together gleefully realising that he was at last making some headway.

'Yes! The posters old man! The posters.'

Knarsnock wrinkled his nose once more in a mouse-like mannerism.

'Tomorrow. Ready tomorrow, Reverend. Ready tomorrow.'

Jasper was just about to open his mouth when Knarsnock, quick as a flash, was by the Reverend's side and with a forcible hand under his arm, pushed him toward the door. Only the Reverend didn't want to leave at that moment.

'Hold on a minute old man,' protested Jasper as he tried to break Knarsnock's vice-like grip.

Knarsnock gave his yellow-toothed smile as he opened the door with his free hand before pushing the Reverend forward.

'Can do no, I am just knocking dem up. You say how? At this moment.'

Jasper's mouth was agog as Knarsnock literally threw him into the street before closing the door behind him. Jasper straightened himself up then noticed a closed sign appear behind the dusty shop window.

'Sneaky is best,' chuckled Knarsnock to himself, as he strode away to his dusty inner sanctum. 'He heee heeee.'

'My God! What a keen fellow. Not even a minute for a chat,' said the Reverend, throwing his leg over his bicycle.

'More power to the fellow. That's what I say,' muttered Jasper as he pedalled off up the high street his belly wobbling to and fro to the rhythm of his pumping legs.

He of the Green name was, as per usual, up at the crack of dawn. With the ending of summer the days had become much shorter. That didn't matter to Green, his day began with the crowing of the cock and if he was awake, everyone was up. Wife, children, even the dog, would be kicked into life to appease the power hungry Green. Though his trade was in vegetables he did like to keep some livestock around. He liked to fuel a green ecosystem where nothing went to waste. Even the hens and pigs were used to compete for the scraps off the Green dinner table.

Not one to see anything go to waste Green found himself with wealth of natural resources, everyone to be exploited to the utmost. His poor long-suffering wife Gwen was little more than a workhorse. She was run from morning to night doing chores outdoors, her housework or anything else that cropped up. She was now a shell of the easy going happy go lucky person she once was. In nature a rose blooms, withers and then is no more, so it was with Mrs Green's marriage. She remained married to the mouldy, compost smelling, brain dead, cabbage-eared horticultural nit twit for the sake of the children. Though she loathed him she was ruled by him. So stingy was Green that when his jumpers started to wear, he made his wife unravel the wool then re-knit the material into socks. If a letter arrived at the house, the children were made to remove the stamps from the envelope, turn the envelope inside out, then paste together the corners so it could be re-used; all be it this time without a stamp. Green knew the stamp would be paid for by the receiver at the other end. Why should he pay for it? Even if the recipient wrote back to complain of his tightness, it would cost them the price of another stamp to do so. It was the only way to do business.

Tight was the operative word when it came to Alec Green. Once when Peter required white socks for P.E. (for he only possessed blue ones knitted from an old blue sweater belonging to his father), Green got some white emulsion paint, dipped the socks in the can, and then left them hanging to dry overnight. Peter could hardly walk during P.E., never mind run, so crusty and hard were his foot covers. To bring matters to a head, as P.E. was held outdoors, lo and behold it started to rain. Peter's socks duly became wet and gave up the suspension of emulsion. The class ran back toward the school from the playing fields with Peter in the middle of the group splashing happily through each puddle he found. Half the pupils entered the changing rooms looking like the human equivalent of a pack of Dalmatian hounds. They were covered in spots of mud intermingled with white patches of emulsion from the socks, which had sprayed around at three hundred and sixty degrees when Peter ran. The culprit was duly spotted as his dark socks were hanging around a pair of green legs, all the emulsion having departed outwards toward his classmates. A letter was quickly dispatched, much to the embarrassment of Peter, asking Mr Green to refrain from experiments in the dying of woollen fabrics and Peter could forthwith wear any color of socks he chose.

'Blooming cheek of the blighters!' said Mr Green at the time. 'Don't they know them socks there were hand knit? The time that was spent by your mother knitting them socks lad. The price you'd pay for something like that in those fancy London stores would cost an arm and a leg. Exquisite is what I call it.'

'Yes dad, sure dad,' replied Peter, glad it was the end of the sock episode and thankful that his father wasn't into painting underpants. Aggh, the pain!

If Gwen Green was farmer Green's bank, for he relied on her heavily, then the children became his reserves. A nest egg, something saved for a rainy day. They too were everyday tools for his use. They could be found in the fields, in all weathers, digging, ploughing, weeding; until the nettles or thistles or sunburn took vengeance and they could return home exhausted, fit only to eat then to bed. He treated his offspring like this but the opposite was true of the great love of his life. His vegetables were treated better than Lords and Ladies. He cared for them, pampered them, and treated them to heat, sunlight and feeding (care of the pigs' manure of course). Vegetables were his true babies, even the odd plant got some attention, but relatives of the human kind came a poor second. Though he worshipped at the throne of his green friends, he was not averse to eating them as it saved on having to buy other food. Succulent!

Don't forget Green's middle name was tight. So much so that he liked to do everything on the cheap, starting with labour. First of all he had his family, which he didn't pay at all, not even a single shilling pocket money for the children. Secondly he was into mechanisation. Because he was on a cheap budget, as in a spend nothing budget, he was always making things. To use a phrase someone once said, these inventions were 'cheap and nasty.' Anyway, Primrose, Peter and mum were to be found, as usual, toiling in the fields while their father locked himself away in his workshop. To the sounds of bang, wallop, rip, 'aaaagghhhhh!' grind, fizzle, 'aaaaaggghhh!' he cut, banged, bloodied himself and his new piece of ingenuity into shape. For all his brilliant ideas a Leonardo Da Vinci of the twentieth-century he most certainly was not, though the inventor and artist of the fifteenth century was who he aspired to be.

It was to be a full two days of bliss for the Green family before he finally surfaced from the workshop. During this time the family did their chores, without his constant nagging, and had some time to themselves. They welcomed time on their own because some sense of normality replaced their ordinarily slavish existence. Emerging from his labours, Alec Green assembled his family in the middle of a field of leeks. The field was composed of sections between furrows where one could walk without damaging the crops. Green had erected several poles which supported curtains of old green tarpaulin. He was evidently using this to hide something. The new invention?

'So I have gathered you all here,' he began with his back to the tarpaulin as he faced his assembly of three.

'Not much choice had we?' thought Primrose.

'To present you with my latest addition to the farming mechanisation industry,' he continued in his air of total arrogance. 'This is an advancement that should bring worldwide recognition to farming, mankind and not least the understanding of perpetual motion. We are living in momentous times......' Green stopped, realising he was

leaving his audience behind, just where they wanted to stay.
'Getting a bit in depth for you three! Physics we're talking
here. More related to an Einstein theory you wouldn't
understand but I can tell you,' he paused giving them one of his
I know it all smiles
'This will save your little legs no end. Heeeee hhhhheeeee.'

The Green family's part of the charade at these MOMENTOUS
TIMES was to stand with mouths agape, as if in awe. In fact, a
lot of times this was the case. Not that Mr Green ever revealed
such secrets of the universe or nature, rather the opposite.
Primrose remembered the last time they stood on the
boundaries of science and nature was when Alec Green's
genius mind thought up the idea of the Methane Powered Self-
Generating Unit, courtesy of untold aromatic dimensions of pig
manure. However, the constraints of gas instead of liquid fuel
were beyond the capabilities of Green and, more to the point,
his converted tractor engine. Luckily the blast that developed
went upwards instead of outwards or else, like the dinosaurs,
the Greens would have become extinct. As it was Mr Green's
roof was blown off his outhouse, as what remained of the self-
generating engine blasted skywards in a ball of flames. An
unfortunate flock of geese that happened to be migrating at the
time were around five thousand feet when they were engulfed

by the gigantic methane burner. Three miles away the villagers of Red Kep leaped with delight as ready cooked geese poured from the heavens. This was probably the first and only gas fired high altitude barbeque ever. However, Alec Green couldn't take the credit for his invention. With the blast and the resulting tremor measuring six point two on the Richter scale in Moscow, Red Kep had been narrowed down as the epicentre. People began pointing the finger at X flight, which operated out of the nearby airbase, having tried some super duper aircraft at zillions of miles per hour. Questions were asked in Parliament about the secrecy surrounding X flight and its high-tech aircraft. Things had gone too far to take any credit for the barbeque and the people of Red Kep weren't complaining. They were eating goose for the next week. Another phenomenon that couldn't be explained, however, was not ten minutes after the geese dropped from the sky it started to rain.........ugghhh......pig manure. This lent more to the saying 'if pigs could fly' than it could to one's imagination.

But all that was behind the mad farmer. Another momentous occasion waited. Alec Green unveiled his curtain to reveal..........what looked like, well...a bundle of scrap. It bore some resemblance to a four-spoked cross that had been mounted horizontally from the top of a pole. The arms that

32

made up the cross were made from steel piping with a series of holes drilled along the length. At the base of the supporting pole emanated part of another pole encasing a rubber garden hose, which ran across the field to an outside water tap. If this contraption was going to lead to the next industrial revolution then Primrose didn't hold out much hope for her father's state of mind. Wow! The man was stark raving bonkers. All she was looking at was a couple of old drainpipes thrown together with a few holes drilled here and there. However, the only thing that drew her attention, and that of her mum and Peter, was the contraption that existed at right angles halfway down the vertical pole. Hmmmm.

'And here we have the overhead spinners which will supply water to the required area,' said Green as he pointed out the intricacies of his machine.

'At ground level you will see the rubber hose water supply suitably encased, so not to be trampled on or sever the supply. As we come up here,' he pointed at the right-angled contraption leading from the vertical pole that closely resembled a truss and yoke arrangement. All that was needed was the power source.

At that moment Peter let out a low groan. Green smiled at his son's dismay. He knew exactly how the others felt. Hee hee

hee, he thought to himself as he let their imaginations run wild for a moment.

'Ah ha,' he said with a mighty roar. 'Caught you all there! He he he,' he said, his eyes widening with a mad look as he revelled in their discomfort. 'You thought you were going to be the power source? Didn't you?'

They nodded in unison, knowing at such times it was better to let him have his little joke and get it over with. Nothing was beyond this idiot thought Mrs Green. She reckoned the remainder of his brain must have been liquefied when his methane machine went skyward. She thought it was about time that the doctors from the asylum were called to end this entire scientific bumpkin once and for all. In the meantime Green was pulling back the remainder of the tarpaulin to reveal his secret propellant!

Primrose let out a gasp of surprise at the small, dark animal her father held on a leash.

'Got the little blighter for nowt,' said her father dragging over what was in fact a Shetland pony. He helped the animal along with a stiff kick up the rear to get it moving in the right direction. He liked animals only slightly less than humans.

'From the pits you know. They like to keep them down there and then'…. He stopped talking as he ground his teeth for effect. 'Then they mince them up for dog meat. Lovely.'

Primrose caught her breath. How horrible she thought, to go through your life half blind and then when you're released into daylight to be tormented by an evil man or worse………to be forced into a tin can. Ugghhh.

'This one seems all right,' said Green as he prodded the Shetland in the ribs. 'A little bony, I grant you, but that's the way I want to keep him. Hungry!'

Well, thought Primrose, it would have to be a call to the Royal Society for the Protection of Cruelty to Animals. Though on inspection, the R.S.P.C.A. would be more likely to lock up her father for being a wild animal than the pony. Peter groaned again as he started to tire of this hullaballoo. He wished his father would dismiss them so they could get on with their work and away from his superior 'know it all,' or more to the point, 'know nothing' attitude.

Green strapped the dark eyed sad little figure of a pony into the contraption.

'This is my power unit. The Mark 1 I'll call it, for it is after all my Mark 1. Haa haa haa,' he said, looking back at his family who feigned some kind of interest.

'Now that we have the power unit....let's supply the fuel. Now where did I put that?' said Green, putting his hands into his coat pockets to appear a few minutes later with a plump carrot which he tied with a piece of string to an old twig.

'There you are. Who could resist one of my prize winning luverlys,' continued the farmer, attaching the twig to the harness so it fell like the bait on a fishing line in front of the Shetland's mouth. He then slapped the pony so hard it jumped about two feet in the air before setting off at an incredible gallop to chase the elusive carrot for eternity. Alec Green stood back to admire his handiwork, but he had forgotten one thing.

'What about the water?' said Peter, watching with absolutely no interest as the pony whizzed round and round like some demented banshee on a fairground ride. Green didn't like to be put on the spot or made to look foolish, the water was just a minor oversight and anyway his workers should be working, not standing round asking him questions. What would they want next? Tea breaks.

'Don't you three worry about the water. There's work to be finished in the fields you know! Better you get up there and get on with it,' said Green fixing his family with his 'don't answer me back' stare. The three turned their backs to him and started to saunter off to finish their relevant tasks.

'Primrose,' he shouted before she got too far out of earshot range.

'Yes,' she shouted back without turning around.

'Could you turn the water on for me?'

'Yes,' she hollered, heading on the direction of the water tap, alone with her thoughts of the beast she called father. What a cruel heartless man to treat an animal like that, especially one that has worked all its days and was now retired, she thought. How would he like to be in the same boat, and dragged out of bed hungry and tired, to trot round a field after a plate of fish and chips with mushy peas which will forever be snatched away. Perpetual motion! Not blooming likely. The lazy old fool.

Just as Primrose turned on the water, she heard the scream. It was unearthly, to say the least. She ran in the direction of the noise, though she knew it could only be her father. Nearing the scene, she realised it was not the emergency she imagined; so she carefully concealed herself behind a bush for cover. The sight was one of pure incredulous hilarity. Mr Green was hanging by the collar of his overcoat from one of the spinners as the pony dragged him round. He was hooked in such a way that his arms were pulled up and he could not reach the buttons to undo his coat. As he shouted, the confusion, noise and the carrot made the pony run all the faster.

Alec Green had managed to stay on his feet, but he resembled some mad, bedraggled scarecrow with a dripping, freezing flow of water down his neck putting him in some distress. He flapped with his arms but to no avail, they remained in midair, but for a second he looked more like crow than scarecrow. All the while the pony cantered on, oblivious to his passenger who was also on the fairground attraction. From her vantage point

Primrose giggled, giggled and giggled some more. After a few minutes she retreated back across the field to finish her chores, leaving her father to continue chasing the pony that he would never catch.

'Oh, things can be so divine when they go wrong,' she thought skipping off to finish her jobs.

It was nearly an hour later when Peter and Primrose assembled around another momentous time in history. They smirked and smiled they talked lowly. Their mother was still on her way there from her distant field.

'Goodness me, he must have come close to world record times,' said Peter his eyes nearly popping out of his head at the scene they witnessed.

Primrose shook her head in disbelief. 'Just what are you talking about Peter?'

Peter seemed to be thinking, 'Well he has probably been running for something like over an hour….and seeing as the pony was trotting at say….maybe ten miles per hour and allowing for him wearing all his clobber, wellies and that. Definitely, definitely, in my opinion he was close to world record times. Hmm, yes.'

Primrose sighed, 'World record what?'

'Pace you know, running, marathons, long distance running. I never knew he was such an athlete, never. Mr Knowles was only telling us the other day about the long distance events and now this, incredible?'

Primrose looked at Peter in amazement. 'The only record he seems to have set is for bog trotting and digging up half the field,' she said, looking at the circular trench and the heap of twisted metal that lay in the centre, with the half conscious form of Alec Green lying like a drowned rat.

Now and then the remains of the perpetual motion monster let forth the odd feeble belch of water as if in the final throws of death. Twisted, broken, no resemblance to the powerful machine it once was, the pony had succeeded in upping the pace, until Green collapsed into the hole he had dug with his wellies as he was dragged round and around. Eventually everything sunk into the trench, breaking the machine in the process. The monster was slain, broken, facing skyward, the pony bolted to new pastures; Green, a casualty in the war to unravel science.

'I've found her,' came the shout from afar.

Peter and Primrose turned in the direction of the shout to see their mother leading the Shetland across the fields. Coming closer, they could see that their mother was feeding the animal with a bunch of carrots.

'She's done herself no harm. Found her grazing away to her heart's content. She must have been really hungry,' said Gwen Green, as she offered the leash to her daughter.

'She must have very good taste then, mother. They are the best carrots in the county after all,' said Primrose, taking the leash and rubbing her hands up the pony's mane. 'There girl, there.'

'Better you take her out of sight, Primrose. It's time to wake up the sleeping giant,' said Mrs Green gesturing with her hand in the direction of Alec Green.

Primrose needed no other words of encouragement; fearing the wrath of her father when he came to his senses. 'Ok I'm off,' she said and was gone.

Gwen Green knew how to work on her husband's ego. She had mastered the technique to such a degree that Alec Green didn't detect her own amusement.

'Come on now, get up,' she said grabbing Green's wet and muddy arm as she helped him up. Peter shook his head as his father stood, slipped, fell, got up, slipped once more until he managed to stand aided by his wife. The antics reminded Peter of a newborn calf trying its legs for the first time. Up, down, up, down, until it finally succeeded.

Peter stayed at a distance from the quagmire as he had seen enough mud and water for one day.

'You're a genius, aren't you? Pure genius,' Gwen Green said, smiling, as she supported her husband by an arm while he continued to slither a little on unsteady legs. What remained of his trousers were on his backside as the fronts were worn away where he had been dragged through the mud. The scarecrow-looking creature was in threadbare, sodden rags, his face a mask of mud from which emanated a pair of bloodshot eyes. Unsteady and fragile, he looked like he would collapse at any moment.

'Pure genius,' repeated Gwen Green once more.

Alec Green wiped away mud from his face as he adjusted his eyes on his wife.

'What are you talking about woman?' he said, holding unto her in case he slipped again. He thought the old goat must have lost the last of her marbles. There he was half drowned, not a stitch to his name, looking more like a cowpat than a human and she was.....was calling him a .....genius? Mad! She was definitely stark raving bonkers.

She continued staring at him in mock hero worship.

'Why, you've gone and made a workout machine!' she said, pointing at the deep trench filled with water.

'Just what I was saying to Primrose, mum,' chipped in Peter. He was trying to lighten the situation a little.

Gwen Green continued, smiling. 'Look, it must be nearly perfect for swimmers. And if we had a more solid foundation I'm sure it would be the ideal aid for the Olympic athlete.'

Alec Green stared at his wife in complete amazement. He was speechless, though not for long.

'Aagh, my leeks, my leeks,' he hollered, clamping his hands over his eyes upon realising that his prize winning crop had been trodden into the mud. 'My leeks, booh hooh,'

'There, there,' said Gwen Green, putting her hand on his shoulder as tears run down his muddy face. 'Sacrifices have to be made in the name of science. You know that better than anyone.' She turned away; certain that if she continued to watch the pathetic sight of Green crying, she would surely burst into laughter.

'Booh hooh booh hooh hooh.'

'Don't worry; their lives haven't been lost in vain. Only the strong survive. Liken this to the experience you had with your hardy perennials when they got frostbitten a few years back. They came back better than ever.' Though she felt foolish she knew she was playing to her husband's ego.

'Sniffle, sniffle,' whimpered Green, straightening himself. 'I...[sniffle sniffle]...suppose you're right. I'll get over it [sniffle]. You've got to lose a battle to win the war [sniffle].'

'And you've proven that your theory about perpetual motion actually works. You've become the guinea pig for a new breed of athletic training aids.' Though she said guinea pig, she thought pig, for her husband looked like a distant cousin of the curly-tailed bogtrotters.

The two crossed the ditch, careful not to put a foot wrong and end up in the manmade, or should that be pony made, swimming pool. Green straightened up as he admired the perfect round perimeter of the ditch. He had vision; he could see the potential there. His composure starting to return, he cleared his throat.

'Yes you're right my dear. How your poor little brain can pick up on my genius I'll never know,' he said, starting to crane his neck as dignity and arrogance once more flowed through his veins.

'Yes, the whole point of this experiment was perpetual motion and I think that I've demonstrated that an athlete could benefit from my sophisticated training course.'

'Perpetual motion my socks dipped in mustard and served in a six month old Gorgonzola cheese sandwich,' thought Peter.

Even a fool knew there was no such thing. You just couldn't get self-sustaining energy without putting something into the equation. The pony provided the power. Like the medieval alchemists who tried to turn lead into gold, perpetual motion was just a myth.

'By the way, woman, where did that pony go?' Green asked, hobbling in the direction of the farmhouse. Gwen Green had to sway him away from any questions on the pony so she ignored the question.

'How on earth did you think of it, anyway?'

Green puffed out his chest with pride, 'Well I just happen to be brainier than the average human. It has always come naturally to me.'

'Yes I can see that,' she said, thinking, 'You're a natural born idiot.'

It was hard being married to the perfect human being. What an ego. Even in failure he found some sort of victory, partly helped by her of course. As they walked, her husband talked but Gwen's mind had escaped to faraway places. She thought of peace, travel and another life.

Peter busied himself cleaning up the mess of the 'perpetual motion machine.' He knew there wouldn't be a mark 2.

Another failure along the same lines would be much too embarrassing, even for his father. In comparison to his Methane Powered Self-Generating Unit, the perpetual motion machine was just....well....tame. What if the old fool tried rocket fuel next or atomic power even? Now that was scary! Peter shuddered at the thought as he set off to find a shovel to fill the ditch.

Chapter 3

Miss Jemima Sally was in her second week at Red Kep Primary School when she had another experience of seeing a flying child. She knew it was her second experience and not a first, since the previous weekend she had made a point of having her eyes re-tested while in London. The optician assured her that her glasses were perfectly suitable and that she did not require stronger lenses. She thought better of telling the optician that she was having apparitions of flying children, as she didn't want to be told that it wasn't her eyesight that needed checking but rather her coconut.

So with her peepers in A1 condition she wasn't about to be fooled into passing it off as an eyesight problem. Cuckoo, maybe, but she would have to eliminate that part of the equation when she saw a shrink. Jemima Sally wasn't imagining the scene, for only twenty minutes earlier she had seen the child at morning assembly. The reason she remembered her, for it was a girl, was the bright red ribbon trailing from her curly locks. The only red ribbon she happened to see that morning. Not green, pink, yellow, brown or purple; definitely red. Other girls may have been wearing ribbons, but the only one that caught Miss Sally's eyes that morning- eyes that were in A1 shape and matched to her perspective lenses she was told- was the girl with the red ribbon. No! Miss Sally was definitely not in the imagination playground.

It all started when she settled the children down to their maths books. Finding the classroom a little stuffy, Miss Sally wandered over to open the window. From her vantage point on the second storey of the school Miss Sally held a perfect view of the west. A small thicket of trees partially obscured her vision of the school playing fields but beyond that the dusty red hill of Red Kep stood out proud against a fluffy white and blue sky. Suddenly from over the tips of the trees sailed an object, its intended trajectory over the top of the school. Such was the closing speed of the ballistic flight path that Miss Sally had only a few scant seconds to realise the unknown missile was, in fact, a girl.

June Daylo was the name to put to the face; a student from Primary Six. The girl with the red ribbon so neatly tied that morning by her over fussy mother who had sent her off to school, unaware that only a short time later the perfect bow and her beloved June would be put through a little wear and tear as she approached an acceleration of nearly six Gs on her first flight into space. Every boffin worth his salt knows that a G represents acceleration due to gravity and that it was first discovered by that wonderful scientist Isaac Newton upon seeing an apple fall from a tree.

June Daylo was putting physical laws into practice. 'What a child!' thought Miss Sally with amazement, as she watched June Daylo encounter air pockets with a built-in natural skill that could only be likened to that of a soaring bird. Right hand down to counter the tumble to port, wings steady....Arms steady, thought Miss Sally mentally correcting herself. Finally young Daylo straightened her flight path. Head now up, with her body straight as a poker, arms clenched by her side as she sought the speed to carry her over the school roof. The tailing red ribbon was the last Miss Sally saw of June Daylo as the young aviator kept her appointment with the larks.

With a shriek of excitement Miss Sally was across the classroom in a flash. Jumping through the door, she opened a window on the corridor, which gave access to the other side of the school. Jemima Sally was intent on witnessing the touchdown. Curious, as children are, first one, then another, then another, trickled out to assume positions by the adjacent windows. Before long the entire class were watching. Miss Sally was oblivious to the children so intent was she on scanning the heavens. 'What in blaze's name is going on?' She asked herself. If she had paused for one minute to ask the children, she may have received an answer. Miss Sally was new to the school but they weren't.

At the beginning there was just a speck but it was quickly growing in size with every passing second, until at last the unmistakable shape of a human body tumbled toward the earth at speed. Miss Sally gasped as she waited for the inevitable. June Daylo about to become an overripe tomato splattered over the lovely green lawns of Red Kep Primary. Aaaaghhhh! Miss Daylo wasn't about to make a montage à la garden for anyone's benefit. With barely ninety feet to go before impact, she found herself in a position head up, feet down. If she could just get rid of the remaining air gap she would be back on terra firma once more. Then, like a black cloud had been lifted on a rainy day, June could see clearly once more. A natural unspoken ability suddenly emerged in the young girl. If anyone ever doubted the Darwinian theory of evolution, it had been poo hayed many, many times; they only had to see Daylo in action to revoke their views.

A phenomenon, to say the least, she clicked into automatic mode with death only inches away. In an instant her arms fanned out, hummingbird fashion, into a flare. It was enough to scrub off the remainder of the speed. For a millisecond the child hung in midair....... just enough time for June to make her move. She didn't hold any belief in any old Darwinian theory that we all emerged from birds. Darwin wasn't stuck fifty feet off the ground and about to encounter the 'what goes up must come down' symptom. It was time to revert back to her human mode of survival so she struck out for anything that was close at hand..........a tall, rather splendid looking fir tree. She made contact in a grabbing bear hug. Saved! Nearly saved. She still had the journey to the bottom to get through. However, evolution had decreed the tree to be perfectly formed for this human flying machine. June slid the whole way to the bottom and was unceremoniously dumped in a bedraggled mess but she was, none the less, in one piece.

'Oh! My goodness,' shrieked Miss Sally as she watched the final death defying moments in pure terror for the mortal life of the flying miracle. As June finally made contact with Mother Earth, a cheer erupted from the entourage of Miss Sally's assembled class. Picking herself up from the ground, June Daylo looked toward the beaming faces of her young audience. In appreciation of their applause, she gave a bow, before walking away across the gardens. Miss Sally noted with some amusement that the girl's red ribbon had remained intact through her ordeal.

For the first time Miss Sally was aware that her class were all hanging like chimpanzees from the school windows. Their shouts managed to wake up all the other pupils from their mundane lessons and a flood of curious bodies, students and teachers alike, pushed their way into the corridor. Owen Wright, young, spotless, pink-fleshed, reeking of cologne, his scrawny neck made even scrawnier by a huge lime green colored kipper tie looped round his throat, was on the scene immediately with his posse of screaming pupils.

'Something up, Miss Sally?' he called out excitedly.

'Nothing to worry about,' answered Miss Sally, feeling slightly embarrassed as she started to shoo her pupils back into class.

'What was the cheer? Who was doing the shouting?' he asked as his pupils jostled around behind their teacher.

'Cricket,' lied Miss Sally, feeling her cheeks flush pink as she said it. Untruths didn't come easily to Miss Sally; but to say she had witnessed a human being flying would only have caused her more embarrassment, so absurd was the idea.

'Cricket!' exclaimed Owen Wright coming closer. His cologne was now so overpowering that Miss Sally was gasping for breath.

'Ugggghh!' she thought, but pointed down to the gardens below.

'Yes, a cricket ball, right over the roof, Mr Wright. It disappeared into the gardens below. My pupils were returning from an excursion and gave a cheer. A sixer, I think you call it,' said Miss Sally, pretending not to know much about the games intricacies.

Bert Eccles was level with Miss Sally. He was the last of her troublesome pupils and she tried to usher him back into the classroom.

'What about the flying Daylo, Miss?' said Eccles, rather too smugly and loudly for Miss Sally's liking.

'Into class, Eccles. There'll be extra lines for you for standing around chattering in corridors. Off you go.' said Miss Sally fixing the lad with a steely stare.

Bert's smile turned into a sulk as he shuffled back into his classroom. Better not to lie when you have witnesses around, thought Miss Sally. She and Bert Eccles were not reading off the same hymn sheet. There is always one who'll drop you in the custard when you least expect it.

'Daylo? One of the Daylo children, are we talking of?' asked Owen Wright, looking straight into Miss Sally's face, trying to detect any air of surprise.

'Daylo? Daylo?' said Miss Sally, pretending to be in thought, 'Ah ha…he means DAYGLO.'

'Dayglo?' said Owen Wright, which gave Miss Sally a few vital moments to think up the next part of her story.

'Dayglo cricket balls. All the rage at the moment! Very easy to find in a thicket and all that. They're luminous little devils, everyone's using them. I'm surprised you haven't heard of them,' babbled Miss Sally, shooting out the words a mile a minute as she tried to get rid of Owen Wright.

'No I haven't,' said Owen matter-of-factly.

'Well I haven't all day to stand here discussing the weather and the cricket form. I have a class to teach, if you don't mind,' said Miss Sally turning sharply on her heel. She was shocked by her own tone of voice and rudeness to a fellow teacher. It wasn't that she didn't like Owen Wright. Aside from his weakness for cheap Cologne, he was a rather friendly, worldly kind of chap. No, Miss Sally had other things on her mind.

'I wonder what bee got in her bonnet,' said Owen Wright as he stared into the air left in the wake of Jemima Sally's disappearance. Giving a sigh of despair he turned back to his pupils.

'Back to class, everyone! That's the excitement over for today.'

Funny thing was Owen had never heard of a dayglo cricket ball. But flying Daylo's, if Miss Sally had mentioned that…now that was an entirely different matter…but Miss Sally was new to the school after all.

With her pupils re-instated in their seats, Miss Sally gave them her most stern face. Well, as stern as she could be. 'Who told you to leave the room?' she demanded.
No answer from the little faces that stared back in their most cherubic form.
'Who?' She repeated, though this time looking at a few individual characters.
'We wondered why you ran out Miss,' said Samantha Bradley, summing up the courage to speak for everyone.
'Well wonder nothing, children,' said Miss Sally, lowering her tone. 'Seems perfectly normal that I was witnessing a landing of some degree of difficulty. Now if you wouldn't mind, please carry on with your maths paper.'

No sooner were the words out of her mouth than Miss Sally found herself in an inner turmoil. Seems perfectly normal that she was witnessing a landing of a rather degree of difficulty…flying schoolgirls! Absolute poppycock! Was she going stark raving mad or had she entered the world of Peter

Pan? She reminded herself that the whole class had witnessed the strange sight so she wasn't alone in her madness. However, there were a few questions she wished to ask the would-be Amy Johnson, and if flying was on the school curriculum then by Jove she wasn't going to be left out of the action. No! She aimed to get to the bottom of this flying nonsense once and for all, 'Right! I'll be back in a minute, children. No one is to leave their seats or there'll be trouble.'

As soon as these words were spoken Miss Sally was out of the door and racing down the corridor at speed. She tackled the staircase three steps at a time. On finally reaching ground level, she burst through the fire escape doors into the grounds on the school's west side. Beyond the trees in the direction of the playing fields, she reminded herself. She was sprinting along at a fair old gallop but where had June gone? Where?

Miss Sally zoomed through the trees to find herself on the playing fields where Mr Knowles was putting his class through a P.E. session. Breathing heavily with the effort of her run, Miss Sally regained her composure by breaking into a brisk walk. With his back toward her, Gavin Knowles wasn't aware of the emergence of Miss Sally onto his hallowed pitch.

Miss Sally knew Gavin Knowles through teacher meetings and thought the man was a bit of a bore. He was always going on about his love of history interlaced with stories about local geographic landmarks where some such battle or event had taken place; the man was very evidently living in the past. If that wasn't enough, his appearance was like that of an army Physical Training instructor; all cropped hair, bulging footballs for arms and a set of shoulders a mile wide which didn't endear him to many. With the appearance of having no neck, his huge deltoids tapered in, like a pyramid, straight to his ears which attached to a miniscule pin sized head. Not even his ears were perfect, one having the vague appearance of a cauliflower, which reminded most people of a mug handle and his head of the rest of the mug. If you thought this looked slightly odd, you only had to go beyond his bulging quadriceps and calves to the man's feet to get a fuller picture. It would be perfectly honest to say his feet were huge, on the dimensions of Coco the clown no less, though if you looked a little closer the similarity ended there. For one, (it was the right foot), appeared to be over twice, yes twice, the width of the other. Definitely the result of some bizarre accident. It looked, to Miss Sally anyway, for she was very attentive, that Mr Knowles was not in fact human but made of rubber. And that when he had been blown up, the air hadn't quite reached the extremities of his left clod hopper, leaving an effect similar to that of a misshapen balloon. Hence the right was always larger. A little more air was all that was required to complete the other foot.

Miss Sally didn't really believe Knowles was a hot air balloon; this was quite evident when his right foot touched earth. More lead than air it seemed as the ground fairly shook under the weight of the gigantic size eighteen. The right foot had an air of menace around it, an aura of foreboding doom mingled with danger. Evil, grotesquely shaped, its power contained within a specially made boot. Shiny, black, polished, gleaming; therein laid the Prince of Darkness. A power of untold dimensions. All in all, Miss Sally concluded that Knowles had not played tiddlywinks in his spare time. She fancied that Knowles was into bear wrestling with the bear being at a distinct disadvantage against the man mountain.

Miss Sally diverted her eyes from Knowles' mud-diggers to his pinhead as he whirled around in her direction. 'Hello Mr Knowles. I was just looking for a girl,' said Miss Sally, catching his eye.
'Take your pick,' Knowles said, offering a hand to show his pupils being put through a series of aerobic exercises. Many of

them seemed fit to drop as the sweat was literally running off them in bucketfuls.

'Oh! It was a particular girl. A girl with a red ribbon,' mused Miss Sally, glancing round, hoping to spy the girl. 'I saw her only a few minutes ago,' she continued.

'Just a moment,' said Knowles, as a boy puffed into view carrying a rugby ball under his arm.

Knowles made an exaggerated motion of clicking the stopwatch, which hung around his ears by a lanyard. The watch should have hung around his neck, but since he didn't possess a neck, it did much better hanging from his ears. Holding the watch in his right hand, he made a loud tutting sound while shaking his head to and fro. With his tongue hanging out, the boy was panting like a dog as he dropped the rugby ball to the ground, waiting for further instructions from his master.

'Don't drop my little beauty like that, Watkins!' bawled Knowles, picking up the ball as gently as if it were a baby and setting it on top of a sports bag. 'I'm the only one allowed to do that, boy. Anyway, you're slower than ever, Watkins! You know the position to assume.' If Watkins tongue was hanging from his mouth before, then it nearly touched his knees now as his jaw dropped.

'But, sir…..' began Watkins, managing to roll his tongue back into its orifice.

'No buts!' interrupted Knowles. 'Assume the position, boy. Now!'

Knowles turned his back to the boy and was blissfully unaware that another student was reaching Watkins a towel. The towel was quickly concealed down the youth's trousers and Watkins pulled out his sweatshirt to camouflage any giveaway of his extra attire. Miss Sally's mouth gaped open as she saw the slight
of hand but as she was at a loss to explain what was going on, she kept mum.

'What was that, Miss Sally?' said Knowles as he caught her look of amazement.

'Nothing,' she quickly replied.

''Scuse me a second,' Knowles responded. He turned back to young Watkins who had now assumed a wrestler type stance. His legs were wide and in a squat. He was slightly bent at the waist, with his head up and his arms hanging by his side. Knowles passed a knowledgeable eye over the boy's structure, allowing himself a smile as he did so. Everything looked perfect. 'Uggghh!' thought Miss Sally, seeing the caricature of a human being's mouth curl up in satisfaction. Heck! Even the man's lips possessed muscles which looked like bent iron girders. Horrible.

'Geography lesson for you, Watkins. So if you get it wrong you're in real trouble.' Meanwhile, the other children took advantage of the situation and slowed their exercises down to a near stop. Not for long though. Nothing escaped the beady eyes of the vigilant Gavin Knowles.

'Who told you horrible lot to stop? Want to join Watkins, do you? If not, get those arms and legs going…..going….going!' he shouted at the top of his voice, causing Jemima Sally to nearly jump out of her skin. Like a giant clockwork machine that has just been rewound, the class sped up once more. Arms up, legs up, jump, squat, starburst, bend over to touch toes……they continued as one in their monotonous routine.

'Right! To start again,' said Knowles, lowering his voice and placing himself to one side of Watkins' plump rear end.

'Geography lesson, Mr Watkins! As I said before, get it wrong then you'll be facing some real trouble! The road next to the village church and running out to the east. I want its name and the distance to the next town. Understood boy?'

'Yes,' whimpered Watkins, his bottom lip trembling.

'Before you depart, remember that for each and every reaction there is an equal and opposite reaction. Now can you tell me who thought that little ditty up, Mr Watkins?'

'Isaac Newton, Sir,' said Watkins, feebly wishing that Knowles would cut the small talk and get on with the ordeal at hand.

'Good,' barked Knowles. 'Just maintain that posture and this will be over in a jiffy. According to Mr Newton's theory this will hurt me far more than it will you, boy.... but don't let that worry you, boy. Have a good one.'

Knowles then expanded his massive chest several times as he gulped in huge amounts of air. Miss Sally was transfixed; he seemed to grow several inches all round, except for the smaller left foot, which stayed the same. His pumping motion didn't seem to extend to his extremities but Knowles had a further few tricks up his sleeve. Twice he slammed the ground with the right-footed Prince of Darkness, the subsequent tremors causing Miss Sally to jump in time to the aerobics class. Knowles then moved into another phase of his ritual.

'Geronimo!' shouted the barbarian schoolteacher causing Miss Sally's hair to stand on end. But this reaction had more to do with the blast of hot air from Knowles lungs, rather than any fear on her behalf. Watkins's card was marked. The war cry was barely finished when Knowles covered the short distance between himself and the boy in two short strides and the Prince of Darkness sliced through air with the dynamic qualities of an anvil. The cushion of air travelling in front of the boot was already pushing Watkins forward as the grotesquely formed foot finally made contact. If there was any noise when leather touched base with Watkins rear no one could say, such was the scream that erupted from the lad's lips it drowned out all other sound and would have put a banshee to shame. Watkins pulled maximum G on take off, though unlike the girl with the red ribbon, he appeared to veer off at an angle from the desired flight path. He was tumbling and falling in the alien environment like children will when they are launched into space. Way over the top of the school, finally disappearing from sight, Watkins' scream hung in the still air long after his mortal body had already begun its descent.

Watkins was not of the flying fraternity. Knowles kicked the ground in disgust, setting off another minor tremor, 'Drat it! Damn foot always lets me down at these crucial moments. Should have taken the blighter on the volley. This would never have happened at twickers. Never!'

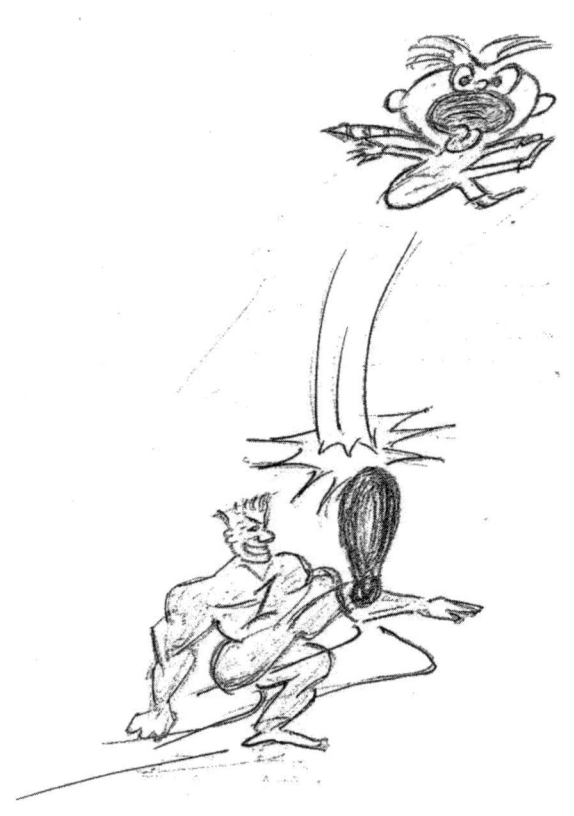

Throughout the entire episode leading up to the launch of
young Watkins Miss Sally had been in a dreamlike state of
surrealism. She was perfectly sure that at any moment she
would awake from this bad dream, to find that she was safely
tucked up in her little bed with all her pleasant knick-knacks
and that the evil menacing Prince of Darkness was just an
illusion. However, with the blood-curdling cry of

'GERONIMO,' followed by a blast of foul air, she finally shrugged off the veil of sleep and returned to reality. The only problem being……….Aaaaghhh…..this was reality! She thanked her lucky stars that Watkins had the good sense to stick a shock absorber down his trunks and she was even more thankful that the volley was relegated to another time when she wouldn't be in attendance. What would Knowles have done? Throw the boy skyward then launch him back into space with a right foot? Where would the 'GERONIMO' war cry fit in? Before or after the volley? Did it really matter? The sum of it all was that Knowles was a monster that thrived on corporal punishment, built around the prowess of his rugby capabilities. How Red Kep Primary allowed such abominable behaviour was beyond Miss Sally.

Knowles approached Miss Sally with a scowl on his face that showed he was still inwardly bitter about his last performance. Never would have happened at twickers remembered Miss Sally.
'Right, old girl. That brat with the red ribbon you mentioned. Miss June Daylo that would be. Causing you some trouble was she?' asked Knowles, an evil grimace spreading across his face. 'Old girl indeed!' thought Miss Sally and her only a sprightly twenty-four! The impertinence of the baboon. What a cheek!

If she had a bucketful of elephant poo at that moment she would have cultivated Knowles' cauliflower-eared pinhead by slipping it over his noggin. Before Miss Sally had the chance to reply, Knowles was already facing his aerobics class and barking out an order.

'June Daylo......out here.....NOW!'

The red ribboned girl bobbed out from the mass of heaving bodies, many of which seemed fit to drop. The only thing keeping them going was the threat of another launch from the dark destroyer. A great incentive to keep.....going ....going....going.

Daylo stood to attention in front of Knowles without the least bit of apprehension or nervousness in her expression. Anyone looking upon June Daylo's relaxed demeanour would think the girl was about to receive a treat, rather than a booting over the school roof. Good girl; she's got it weighed off thought Miss Sally. Show absolutely no fear, and then rely on your pre-flight plan to get you out of trouble. Natural instinct. Don't let the bully get you down, girl.

'Causing trouble again Daylo?' bawled Knowles, staring down at the petite and pretty Daylo child. 'I think I have another lesson coming up for you girl.' Knowles gave an evil smile, 'Geography.' The word should have been enough to send a tremor through a normal child's body but not June Daylo's. She remained cool and aloof. However, Miss Sally did not wish to sanction another flight for the girl that morning, no matter how much the child loved soaring with the birds. Miss Sally straightened her glasses and cleared her throat as she searched for an excuse to save Daylo's skin from another encounter with the elements of heaven and earth.

'It's nothing like that, Mr Knowles. I only wanted to ask June where she acquired the beautiful red ribbon she is wearing this morning.' said Miss Sally, addressing June, then looking to Gavin Knowles whose face sagged in dismay. 'I'd rather like that color for my flower arranging bouquets.' continued Miss Sally with a cheerful smile. Knowles did a double take, first looking at the girl, then back to Miss Sally. He couldn't believe what he was hearing. Flower arranging, ribbons......she was disrupting his class because of a few weeds tied together with a bit of string. It seemed Miss Sally needed a spot of guidance.

'Are you sure she hasn't been in trouble. Maybe just a little bit. Give you the look or something?'

Miss Sally shook her head, still smiling. Knowles nostrils flared angrily.

'Well maybe you don't like the color of her hair?'

Miss Sally continued smiling as she shook her head in response to the bully's questioning. Knowles raised his finger as his nostrils flared once more, not unlike a bull. 'I've got one for you...ah ha...the color of her eyes doesn't match the color of the ribbon and it makes you want to puke. There's one for you,' shouted Knowles, clapping his hands together in glee. 'That'll teach the little brat. Heee....heeee...heee. What do you think Miss Sally?'

Miss Sally continued with her fake smile. 'Oh, you can be so funny and childish at times Mr Knowles,' said Miss Sally. Giving a mock laugh and ignoring Knowles, she turned to June. 'Where did you get that ribbon, June?'

'Answer Miss Sally, girl!' yelled Knowles, as he bristled at the putdown from the junior teacher. Childish indeed, he would show her, but first he wanted to give Daylo 'one for the road' just to let the little brat know who was in charge.

'From Leckeys Stores in the High street Miss,' said June Daylo, letting slip a smile for the rather nice Miss Jemima Sally.

'Thanks,' replied Miss Sally. She was glad that she had managed to keep the girl on terra firma by using the right choice of words to the knuckle dragger without infuriating him too much.

'Well don't stand there cutting the cake, girl!' bawled Knowles and as soon as the words were spoken the girl was back among the sea of bodies. 'Got to keep the little blighters in check. Give them an inch and they'll take a mile. Discipline is what's needed here. That's what these little brats understand. They don't forget that in a hurry.' mumbled Knowles, sorely grieved at missing out on another geography extravaganza by way of Miss Sally's humanity. As he grumbled Knowles subconsciously tapped the ground with his size eighteen youth launcher.

Miss Sally had seen enough of flying geography trained students for one day, besides; her own pupils would be causing mayhem in her absence. Such was the way of the young, when the cat's away the mice will play. Time to be getting back, she thought.

'Thanks very much Mr Knowles. I hope young Watkins isn't too late in returning from his field excursion.' As she said it Miss Sally hoped the boy had enjoyed a safe landing. Knowles grunted something in return but Miss Sally didn't hear she was already on her way. Knowles reached down to retrieve his precious rugby ball from its position on top of his sports bag where it rested like an egg in the protection of a nest. He touched the leather of the ball where five deep gouges existed against the otherwise smooth exterior of the ball. At times like this holding his 'baby' helped him relax; they had been through so much together…..the power and the glory……the pain and the suffering. He snapped back to reality with a thought on Jemima Sally. She was going to be trouble that one. He could tell…..very troublesome.

Miss Sally made up her mind while on the way back to class that a visit would have to be paid to the school principal concerning some of the strange goings on that were being accepted as the norm. The Wright brothers, those pioneers of the first powered flight, would turn in their graves if they could see how easily Knowles defied the laws of nature with his size eighteens in his quest to get a person airborne. What would he be doing next? Offering one way flights into the next county with a free geography lesson thrown in- all for six penny a throw at the upcoming local church's flower and veg show. Roll up, roll up! Miss Sally dismissed the thought quickly. Once a few adults got wind of Mr Knowles wrong doings his astrological guide would need re-reading with regard his job prospects. In the meantime she thought some of the gentler arts needed to be introduced at the school. It would provide a sense of escapism for some of the children.

Miss Sally entered a classroom to find children in different seats, paper aeroplanes flying around, lobbed paper clips, raspberries being blown, shouts, books being thrown. Much as any unattended classroom would be. After her adventures with Mr Knowles, Miss Sally's feathers weren't ruffled one bit. 'Back to your seats,' she said firmly but quietly. As the circus started to disintegrate she noticed that the hair girl, Primrose Green, seated at the rear of the room, stared out of a window completely oblivious to all that surrounded her. Jemima Sally made up her mind to try and touch base with this girl. Something wasn't right there but maybe she could help. She sighed. Perhaps she was just a stupid, doddering daydreamer after all. How did she expect children to enjoy school when they were likely to encounter people like Mr Knowles, who were only too likely to kick them into touch because their teeth weren't the same color as his polished black boots? What a place indeed. Yes, Red Kep needed a little more love and humanity injected into the village. She hoped for the future.

Chapter 4

Miss Sally was aware from day one that Primrose Green was somehow different from her classmates. Nothing to do with the fact that she walked around with more blooms in her hair than could be found at the Chelsea Flower Show or that the girl was ever so slightly green. These things Miss Sally overlooked as she sought to find the spiritual side of Primrose. There was a quality, though she couldn't quite put her finger on it, a gift if you will that Primrose had in abundance that none of the other children possessed. To be truthful the other children all had their own unique characters and talents, as have all children, but these substances were evident. The brick wall that Miss Sally faced was that she couldn't fathom the capabilities of Primrose Green. Here was a deep bottomless ocean, an elusive Holy Grail, yet to be discovered. Miss Sally's intuition told her that there was more to the child than a thatch full of Rhododendrons.

'Hair is green. Face is green. Her name is Green. Frogs are green.......She thinks she's a fairy queen but everyone knows.......NA NA NA NANA. Green is the color of ......PUKE.' Miss Sally's super sensitive lugs picked up the continuous chant from across the playground. She didn't need

two guesses to realise to whom the horrible remarks were being
directed. With rescue in mind, she set off in pursuit of the
aggressors.

The scene was of half a dozen children clasping hands as they
danced around the girl seated in their midst. They seemed to be
having a fabulous old time as they chanted and jigged in
warlike tribal fashion, leering at their prey.
'Children,' called out Miss Sally as she got within a few feet of
the group.
'Miss Sally!' screamed Sarah Young, spying her teacher
bearing down on them.

Like an exploding firework the bunch of excited, tittering kids fragmented; disappearing into every nook, cranny and corner of the playground as they tried to put some distance between themselves, their hostage, and the knight in shining armour.

'Are you all right, Primrose?' asked Miss Sally, looking at the girl who sat cross-legged on the ground. Primrose's hands rested on her frock, clutched tightly together as if in prayer. Her violet eyes fluttered open as if awakening from a dream. She seemed completely unfazed by the threatening ordeal she had been subjected to.

'What have you got there?' asked Miss Sally, her curiosity getting the better of her.

'A frog Miss,' replied Primrose, uncupping her hands a fraction of an inch to give her teacher a view of her resident. A little green head emerged from the safety of his human minder to look at the hostile outside world, which somehow looked a little better since the war party had departed. Primrose smiled at the frog, 'I was just trying to protect him from the others. You know how horrible the boys can be to small creatures. You never know what they might do.'

Miss Sally didn't particularly like frogs either, but she couldn't stand children who were hurtful to animals. Primrose was certainly a Samaritan to her less fortunate friend.

The school bell chimed out to signal the end of lunch break.

'There you go Primrose,' said Miss Sally. 'Your cue to let the little feller go.'

Ever so gently Primrose uncupped her hands to let the little frog leap onto the grass below. With a last glance around his surroundings, he kicked with his bow legs and sailed through the air into the longer grass beyond. The girl gave a contented smile, knowing that the frog was now safe from further harm, at least for the moment.

Primrose clambered to her feet to walk alongside Miss Sally back toward the school

'So you like animals?' ventured Miss Sally, hoping that she had finally broken the ice between herself and the flower child.

'Yes I do, Miss Sally. I always find I have time for other creatures. It's just that sometimes…..' she hesitated. 'Oh, it doesn't matter,' finished Primrose, feeling that she was revealing a little too much of herself to her teacher. Miss Sally stopped walking, as did Primrose.

'Go ahead. You can tell me anything, Primrose. I can keep a secret you know.' she said, lowering her voice to emphasise her sincerity.

Primrose bit the bottom of her blood red lips hard, making the skin turn white as she thought over Miss Sally's proposal. Her teacher seemed all right after all. Kind and generous, maybe she could let her into her head, just a little. She released her bottom lip from the grip of her incisors, allowing the blood to return once more. The girl glanced around suspiciously, hoping that no one was within earshot of what she was about to reveal.

'Please promise you won't tell another soul. People think I'm strange already you see.' Yes, Miss Sally could certainly agree with that statement. The botanical garden cultured hairdo, upon a green coconut, certainly wasn't typical of the pupils of Red Kep Primary. Pleasantly different though, thought Miss Sally. An eye-catching piece of originality and individuality which when gazed upon would never be forgotten to the eye of the beholder. Primrose Green was most definitely memorable.

'Is that because you're a little green?' said Miss Sally, with some caution so as not to cause any offence. 'A little different from the other children? I don't see much difference myself. What's a little bit of color here and there?'

Primrose was starting to warm to Miss Sally. The teacher had a better perception than others, who instead regarded the girl as some freak of nature.

'That's exactly what I think, Miss. It's all really because of my diet. You see I eat far too many greens and this is the result,' said Primrose, with a shrug of her shoulders before adding, 'green.'

'Hhhmmm,' mused Miss Sally, 'and everyone is telling us to shovel all those good old veggies down our gullet. Good for the body and all that bumpkin.'

Primrose gave a sigh. 'There's a bit of a difference between a spoonful and a bucketful, Miss. I should know after working in the fields….'

'You're working, girl!' exclaimed Miss Sally, a look of amazement spreading across her face.

Primrose's eyes darted towards the ground. 'Just a little…only sometimes,' lied Primrose trying to backtrack on her last statement.

Little wonder the girl always looked so removed, distant from the rest of her classmates. Miss Sally reckoned the girl was exhausted from overwork, always appearing only half awake in school. Was this her secret?

'Do you want to tell me about this work that you're doing?' said Miss Sally trying to coax a response from her pupil.

'I told you I don't work much,' snapped Primrose in reply, trying to bury the subject once and for all.

Miss Sally knew when to drop a hot potato. She sensed, however, she would have to tread carefully or Primrose would think of her as an interfering busybody to be avoided at all costs. Not something she wished to happen after finally breaking through the girl's outer barriers. 'Oh, alright then. What was that other thing you wanted to tell me about? Your secret.'

'That can wait till another time, Miss,' was all that Miss Sally heard, as Primrose skipped off in the direction of the school doors.

Frustrated, Miss Sally stamped her foot on the ground. 'Drat!' Just when she had opened the door to the inner Primrose Green, she had slipped on a ripe banana skin and slammed the door closed in the process. Still, there would be other opportunities. She would just have to bide her time for another moment.

Reverend Jasper slipped through the gate and out of the churchyard. Walking beside his cycle he paused on the roadside to look up at the huge oak tree where only that morning he had seen young Watkins making like a demented chimpanzee with two dislocated shoulders. Up the wrong tree for chestnuts and a bit early in the season, he had thought at the time and so he decided to investigate further. However,

Watkins wasn't hanging around and made off at a fast rate of knots toward Red Kep. Should have been at school anyway, the little blighter, thought the reverend as he viewed the fleeing form of Watkins leaving a trail of leaves and twigs in his wake.

Anyway, that was this morning. Jasper had other things to attend to. Climbing aboard his cycle he was soon pumping his legs as the swing of his belly tried to catch up to the rhythm. He covered the short distance in a matter of minutes. He then dismounted the cycle, as was his routine and walked through the village, meeting members of the community.

'Afternoon, Reverend Jasper. Not long to the big show now,' said Joe Biggs, a local horticulturist of some renown in his chosen field of creeping plants.

'Bout eight days left Joe. Got any old favourites lined up?'

'I've always thought that we should have the show in the summertime, Reverend. It would mean that we could show off some of our earlier blooms.'

'We're catering more for the late comers and the veg at this time of the year. That's the way the locals like it. Do you mean to tell me you have no entrants this year, Joe?'

Joe touched the side of his nose with his finger in a knowledgeable manner. 'Always something in the pot, Reverend. Better to leave the competition guessing up to the last minute! You know how things can mysteriously occur at this time of the year.'

Jasper nodded his head in agreement, 'I know what you mean Joe. It's best to keep your cards close to your chest.'

'See you later then,' said Joe, as Jasper continued on his way.

Reverend Jelly Belly knew only too well what Joe Biggs hinted at. It was a fact of village life that a lot of unusual happenings always occurred in the lead up to the big event of the year. Amazon sized slugs and caterpillars, magicked away from some zoo or other, tended to appear in cabbage patches overnight and leave them stripped to the roots by morning. There were cattle or goats that were able to unlock gates and dogs that liked digging up flowerbeds in their hunt for bones. Yes! The Reverend Jasper had heard it all before. He used to think it was only healthy competition but now things were going too far. Nobbling was the proper terminology to use for his parishioners' sleight of hand; they were professionals in the art of nobbling... Heck, people were even camping out in their plots overnight as if they had come across a gold strike. How devious one could be in their ploy to get a simple rosette. There was nasty and then there was sneaky nasty.

'Hello, Mrs Knot,' said the Reverend in greeting to another member of his flock. She was seldom called Mrs Knot these days. With her husband long since passed on, the mother of four and grandmother to eight much preferred the Granny Knot handle used by many of her fellow villagers. Less formal, perfectly suited to her look, plain old Granny Knot.

'Hello, Reverend Jasper.' She pulled on the brakes of her rickety, rusty, antique pram. It was her means of transporting goodies for her little jaunts around the area, ideal for her means as an avid campaigner for charity as well as her role as Major in the local Salvation Army. The perambulator was a work horse, carrying to and fro everything from clothes to foodstuffs for the less well off. Seventy years of age, Granny Knot's face was weather-beaten to the extent that it resembled a dried out prune. Her sally army uniform, which she nearly always wore, was so immaculately pressed you could peel a potato off the edge and her shoes were buffed to a mirror-like finish.

'What have you got there, dear,' was Jasper's invitation for a nosey as he peeked inside the pram. Granny Knot smiled showing more ripples than a pebble landing in a still pond. The Reverend felt himself getting slightly seasick.

'A few old clothes I've been collecting for the inner-city homeless. Everyone has something lying around that they've grown out of,' she said, giving an unintentional glance at the super tight pullover stretched over the Reverend's quivering belly. The Reverend sucked in his stomach, pulling down his pullover.

'I know what you mean. Now have you got anything for the horticultural extravaganza coming up?'

She smiled again. Rippling. 'I'm thinking of setting up a stall selling some of my preserves. The old favourites....gooseberry...blackberry...strawberry.'

The Reverend Jasper licked his lips in anticipation as his jumper started to ride up his belly once more. 'Sounds nice to me. Hmmmm....hhmmm,' he said, pulling the tight garment over his fleshy pot once more.

'Well excuse me, Mrs Knot. I really am in a bit of a rush this afternoon. I've got to go and meet old thingy-ma-jig.'

'Give him my regards then,' called out the grandmother, moving off.

'Thingy-ma-jig, of course,' she shouted with a laugh, which caused a tidal wave of ripples on her face.

'Good one....good one,' laughed Jasper catching the joke.

He set off for his final call. Knarsnock's.

Jasper opened the door, to be announced by the ringing of a bell. He thought he could detect a succession of bells but put the acoustics down to an echo somewhere in the bare interior. Upon entering, B.J.B. adjusted his eyes to the nocturnal lighting which was Knarsnock's trademark. He whistled to himself as he awaited the arrival of the printing master, from whatever project he was currently engaged upon within the confines of his inner sanctum. It was so dark looking into the interior workshops, that Jasper thought he'd set foot in a coalbunker. The little fellow must save a fortune on electricity thought Jasper, looking around for anything resembling a light bulb. A door opened, closed, and then Knarsnock appeared out of the gloomy and dusty interior.

'Goodness me,' gasped Jasper, his eyes getting accustomed to the dinginess and the appearance of the Norwegian. Knarsnock was covered from head to foot in a layer of red dust. His eyes looked like two fog lights but he squinted like a mole to see in the semi darkness.

'Vat,' said Knarsnock, coming closer.

'You really should get someone in to help you out with a spot of dusting, old man! You seem to be having a bit of a problem in here.' Finishing the sentence, Jasper leaned over to blow a layer of dust from the smaller man's shoulder. He watched in amazement as the dust caught what little light was in the room, changing into a hundred tints as it flew away, before eventually fading from view.

'Some paint color powder I'm trying out, so,' Knarsnock smiled, his usually yellow teeth taking on the hue of red.

Jasper took one step back. The little fellow bore more resemblance to a vampire than a printer. Not that he had ever seen a vampire, but if the bloodthirsty critters did exist then he was sure Knarsnock would pass as a not too distant cousin. The Norwegian's nocturnal habits were leading him into the realms of the supernatural.

'It must be a fair old batch you're mixing. That's quite a big thingy you got there.' Jasper was looking at a huge dusty, red shovel resting against a wall.

'Yes,' replied Knarsnock, twiddling with his moustache, trying to get the dust from his bristles. This only served to agitate the dust even more, causing Knarsnock to sneeze, shooting out two red looking lasers from his nose.

'Is that a bit of pasta hanging from…?' Jasper didn't finish the sentence since Knarsnock disappeared behind his huge counter and began to rustle around. He appeared a short time later to dump a box of leaflets on the countertop.

'What you're after this'll be,' which really meant 'this'll be what you're after.'

'The thingies. Yes, of course,' said Jasper, accepting the leaflets and posters for the upcoming show.

Just as Jasper stowed the package under his arm a resounding boom could be heard high above the village, causing the glass panes to rattle in Knarsnock's and many other Red Kep dwellings. Knarsnock's green eyes showed a tingle of excitement.

'A change in the weather must be coming. Electrical storm, thinking I,' said Knarsnock, once again losing something in the translation. Jasper cocked his head to the side as he caught the last of the low rumbling sound.

'Sounded more like one of those new military jets from the airbase. The super fast thingy-ma-something they're all talking about.'

'Think so I don't,' said Knarsnock, placing his hand under Jasper's arm as he guided the Reverend toward the door. Upon opening the door, Knarsnock distracted the Reverend by looking up at the ever-darkening sky.

'See that thunderstorm big up there?' he asked.

Jasper looked skyward, but after leaving the rabbit warren that was Knarsnock's shop, he was blinded by the brightness. He squinted several times as his eyes readjusted to daylight. Knarsnock was already closing the door.

'Hold on Mr Knarsnock. I haven't paid you yet,' cried Jasper, turning back to the door but finding it already locked. Jasper shook his head in amazement then started to talk to himself, 'Strange little fellow. Always rushing around and keeping the oddest hours. Becoming more slippery than an eel covered in baby oil. And that piece of pasta hanging from his ear.........now that I think about it, it looked more like a worm. Weird.' Still talking to himself, Jasper deposited his goodies into his bicycle basket before setting off on further errands.

Chapter 5

Knarsnock was correct. Somewhere out there in the heavens a storm was brewing, but it was not to be any old storm. Not the kind of storm that makes you want to jump into bed and pull your duvet over head as the wind, rain and hail beat relentlessly against your window, threatening to blow your roof off even though it never does. This was not to be a storm of climatic fronts fighting for their place; cold air clashing with hot air in a competition to see who was stronger. No! The storm would be far more than that. This storm originated from much further afield. A cosmos storm no less. One that Red Kep would never forget. Ever.

Primrose trooped the last few steps toward the rusty shack that overlooked the vegetable field. She had just visited Pippa; the Shetland pony saved from the clutches of her father had been given a name by her. Her father allowed the girl to care for the animal while he thought up a further use for the pony, though he frequently reminded her that there was always the canine clientele waiting in the wings. Primrose envisaged releasing the pony before that day arrived or reporting her father to the RSPCA. The latter idea seemed a better proposition. Primrose stood outside the doorless shed, exposed to the elements. It was almost dusk.

Peter waited impatiently for his sister's arrival.

'Tough that you drew the short straw for the night shift,' remarked Peter, looking out at the encroaching night. 'It gets kind of spooky out here when those ghoulies and monsters start creeping around. Sppppooooooookkkkkkyyyyyyy.'

Primrose was nonchalant, 'Don't waste your breath. Mum's got your tea on the table and the old boy'll be in soon, so you'd better report in.'

'Ok, I'm off, but…Peter's blue eyes widened, accentuating his luminous green face and making him appear eerie. Don't be afraid of the…..AAAWWWWOOOHHHH.'

The howl echoed around the still countryside. Primrose laughed. She wasn't about to let him instil fear into her.

Peter smiled, 'Worth a try anyway. See you.'

'See you,' called out Primrose, as Peter skipped off under an ever darkening sky, howling as he travelled.

In trying to put the frighteners on his sister, Peter had only succeeded in spooking himself. To the extent that he kept glancing over his shoulder to see if he was being followed. Peter's bravado about the dark was only a cover for his own fear. His pace increased…his glances became more frequent…. until, finally in his flight for home…he broke into a fully fledged run. We all know how one's imagination can get the better of one. In reality there was nothing out there. Primrose sat in the shed quite content as the coming of the descending darkness covered her like a blanket. Anyway, just to be on the safe side, she kept her little flashlight close by. Though she was not afraid of the night, she was painfully aware that she shouldn't be caught out in the open with an approaching storm and the likelihood of lightning.

Her makeshift seat was a very comfortable hay bale. Primrose closed her eyes, not to sleep but to make better use of her senses. Being a flower child, she loved the sounds of nature. A far-off bird squawking, the slither of a newt through wet grass, the trickle of stream water over rocks, the bark of a nervous dog….all carried further on night air, without the interference of daytime sounds. Much better than all of these….much, much better, was her favourite…..the sound of the wind. She imagined some great giant sleeping outdoors in a far-off land, the rise and fall of his chest causing a gentle breeze. He was peaceful, sleeping.

She was aware of the increasing intensity of the wind as the leaves rustled, trees swayed and the shed's timbers creaked.

With the first rumble of thunder she felt her breath being sucked from her lungs. The giant was now awake and angry. With more rumbling in the air there came the sound of a single drop of rain falling on the roof. Several more drops fell, until the downpour properly started. Rain belted off the roof like a thousand drummers playing simultaneously. A little rain blew through the open front of her shelter but she felt relatively secure. The wind increased and a thousand more drummers joined the ensemble, the shed straining and creaking in sympathy with the rhythm. Still the girl felt safe. The streaks of lightning heralded the presence of thunder and vice versa. The night sky became like daylight. As the storm reached its zenith above the shed, a new sound invaded Primrose's razor sharp hearing. The ever-increasing high-pitched whistle made Primrose's curiosity get the better of her. Stepping outside she saw a break in the dark skies.

Looking toward the heavens she could identify the reason for the whistle. A speck of brightness, increasing in size, trailed a fleck of fire in its wake as it fell with a magnetic like attraction straight toward her position. A meteorite, she realised excitedly. In a second her sense of excitement was replaced by fear. There was nowhere to run as the speck became a ball of fire eating up the distance between itself and Primrose. The shriek of the whistle drowned out the sound of the storm. Primrose found herself rooted to the ground, unable to move. It is said one should wish upon a falling star.....perhaps Primrose should have used her wish to avert the disaster, but so spellbound was she by the sight and sound that she couldn't think straight. What she needed was a......miracle.

If a miracle was Primrose Green's wish, then a miracle she would have. With the storm right over her position, a bolt of lightning shot out from the enraged heavens searching for earthbound matter for contact. By some strange sequence of events the precise trigonometry of both lightning and meteorite led both to try filling the same time in space. A scant few feet above her head, the resultant explosion was both deafening and intense in its brilliance. It looked like a huge firework separating into a billion sparklers destined to go their different directions toward earth.

Primrose's first reaction was to cover her face with a hand, shielding her eyes from the intense light but she didn't want to miss any moment of the wondrous phenomenon. Upon removing her hand she was greeted by a magical silence. Glowing, miniscule parts of material danced around like fireflies in the electrified static of the air, before falling to earth.

She watched as a sparkle dropped off the end of her nose, flying off to mingle with its other phosphorescent friends. Primrose felt oh so different. Queer but not frightened. Not afraid at all. She watched with intrigue as the sparkles started to fade away, noticing that one particular sparkle fell onto the patch by her feet. If she felt strange before, then what she was about to witness made that seem very normal indeed.

'Oh no! No! It's all gone,' cried Alec Green at the top of his voice, as he used a little flashlight to stare across a scorched field, devoid of any vegetation. With a trembling hand he lifted a few tatty shreds of a brussels sprout leaf.
'That's all that's left....that's all! All my hard work gone to waste. Boo...hoooh...hooh...my little darlings...my babies.'
Primrose looked on the scene with mild amusement. She felt like laughing, but since her father was in mourning she put the idea to the back of her mind. How ridiculous he looked, she thought, a grown man crying over a few soggy leaves. Really.
'There's a few peas here as well, Dad,' she chirped up, looking at the peas she was trampling over. 'Well you could call them mushy peas, I suppose.' Primrose surprised herself by speaking up, but after her 'EXPERIENCE' she didn't much care if she upset her father or not. He hadn't so much as enquired about her wellbeing after the storm. Instead, he was

more concerned about the disappearance of his precious crops, his little 'babies,' the 'little darlings.' Ughhh! It was enough to make her sick.

'The police, Primrose. Back to the house quickly, girl. We'll get the police after the blighters. They can't have gone far. Quickly.'

Primrose followed the bobbing trail of the flashlight as the green-fingered doddering fool set off back toward the house ranting and raving of how professional the thieves had been.

Alec Green banged the phone down with frustration, 'Drat, those rascals have cut the line. Real pros. Stole the best of my brussels, not to mention my other little beauties, and then they cut my phone line! They'll be halfway to the next county before I can notify the authorities. The death penalty is what we need for them varmints. Stealing people's foodstuffs like that. The death penalty for the brussels theft and life imprisonment for cutting the phone lines. It shouldn't be allowed. Blinking country, what is it coming to?'

'The phone being cut off......has that anything to do with you not paying the bill?' The voice belonged to Primrose; she didn't really know she had said the words, only that she had thought them. Alec Green's nostrils flared like two jet air intakes as he sucked in air, dust and insects. He looked around for the deliverer of the sentence. He stared upon the remainder of his family with complete disbelief. No one dared to talk to him like that. Ever.

'Who said that?'

No reply came from the other Green family members. Primrose was sure she hadn't said the words only thought them. Perhaps her father was able to read minds now. Would the thought of a chocolate bar qualify for the death sentence followed by life imprisonment? She was sure life imprisonment followed by the death sentence made a lot more sense or the death sentence followed by release from prison or......anyway none of it made any sense it was her father after all. The lack of response from the others was too much for Green. Here was a man who hated repeating himself. When he asked a question he wanted a response.

'Who said it?' he bawled.

'Are you deaf as well as stupid,' came back the lightning reply.

Though Alec Green asked the question, he never envisaged this response. To disrespect him once was absolute folly.... but twice was suicide. Primrose recognised the voice as her own but it was somewhat ghostly...floating, not under her control. She looked away from her father, toward Peter and her mother. They seemed frozen in time, their mouths hanging aghast.

Primrose wondered if this was shock. Had they too heard the strange, disembodied voice so like her own. Yes! They certainly had.

Gwen Green wanted to scream, 'Are you a currant short of a fruit cake, girl. Waken up!' But no words came out. Like Peter she was struck dumb by Primrose's recklessness. As if in a dream, Primrose glanced around the room for some answer to this dilemma. Was there a ventriloquist at work? It seemed not. What was going on? The sweep of her eye once more met her father's. Could she apologise at this stage? By the look of his face that option was already ruled out. Primrose had heard of out of body experiences but never an out of voice experience. What strange forces were at work? Facing her father Primrose did what she thought best in the circumstances. Smiled. At least that was better than saying something. Mr Green's reply was to snarl. The tiny blood vessels in his eyes bulged like boa constrictors trying to escape. The man had reached saturation point.

'Something funny, girl? You think all this is so funny......that my sprouts have been....been kidnapped.'

'Sprout napped' replied Primrose once again not in control of her own voice.

A low groan was all that Gwen Green could muster. Her daughter had definitely flipped; this was so out of character for the child. Meanwhile her husband simmered like an overripe volcano about to blow its top as he loomed over Primrose. 'Sprout napped!' he yelled, pointing a menacing finger into Primrose's face. 'You were there, girl. You saw it all...assist the blighters did you? Shovel my little lovelies up then pack them off in a truck. Did you help them torch the ground to make it look like a lightning strike? Cover up your tracks...huh? You wretched brat....answer me!' The mouldy compost covered filthy finger waved around in front of Primrose's face in a threatening manner. Just at the right moment she opened her mouth, sinking her teeth into the vile object.

'Aaaaghhh' yelled Green feeling the super strong incisors that had never touched a sweet grind through the flesh of his finger to reach the bone. If her father felt the impact then it wasn't so nice for Primrose either. Her taste buds went into overload as they likened the fusty green finger to a six-month-old kipper served on a bed of a cowpat. Gagging for a breath, she had to release the pressure. It was enough for Green to get away with his finger intact. He wouldn't make the same mistake again.

Keeping his hands away from the girl's mouth he grabbed her
by the shoulders and started to shake.

Up to that point Primrose had been trying to stay in control.
Sure the voice thing had thrown her but she was learning to
cope with that. If she thought something it just seemed to come
out. There was no ventriloquist hiding in the corner, she was
the one speaking. If she didn't think anything then she
wouldn't say anything. Simple. However, the shaking was to
unleash another dimension to Primrose. She had taken enough
of this idiot who cared more about a few limp lettuce leaves
than about the welfare of his own family. Instead of the usual
meek, mild Primrose Green, her father was about to unleash the
thorny, jagged, nasty Primrose Green.

Somewhere deep inside her brain a switch was triggered. Most
young girls, or boys for that matter, when frightened naturally
cry, scream or make some kind of noise. So it was for
Primrose. It seemed the most natural thing in the world to open
her mouth and......Mr Green dropped the girl like a red-hot
anvil. At the same time he clamped both hands over his ears
and sunk to his knees. What emitted from the mouth of
Primrose was no scream but the rumble of an earthquake, low
in frequency but high in volume. To Alec Green it felt like a

train was running through the middle of his skull. He had never known so bad a headache, not even when he had thrown his prize winning twenty-pound melon above his head in jubilation at winning a rosette, only to miss the catch letting the fruit splatter on his head. Even the resulting fall from the plinth into the spectators was without pain since Green was already in the land of daydreams, splattered from head to foot in gooey melon innards. Being unconscious upon hitting the ground, he couldn't appreciate the rapturous applause from the crowd with no one more jubilant than his darling wife. Coming to over an hour later in hospital with a tomato sized bump for company, it was to be a further week before he lost the double vision and nearly a month before his skull regained its original shape. A good month for the rest of the Green family.

Yes, Alec Green had the headache to end all headaches. His headache sounded like a train and he absolutely despised trains. Horrible smelly, noisy, running at all hours of the day or night they cut up good fertile land which could be put to much better use. However, this train wasn't running through the countryside....it was running through the middle of his cranium.

'CHUG...CHUG...CHUG...BUMO...BUMO...BUMO...'
Green's face showed the intense pain and he tried to keep the

sound out by keeping his hands over his ears. All was in vain, for the sound was already inside his head. If Alec Green was immobilised, then his son was the opposite. Fearing for his life the boy reacted.

'Runaway train,' shouted Peter, diving for cover under the kitchen table. He was joined seconds later by his mother, as the walls and ground vibrated to the oncoming iron behemoth…'CHUG...CHUG ...CHUG...BUMO...BUMO...BUMO.' The house trembled on its foundations. Alec Green trembled on the floor and his straining bloodshot eyes threatened to pop out like two champagne corks. Gwen and Peter trembled under the kitchen table. Still the runaway train bore down threatening to burst through the walls of the farmhouse at any moment, demolishing everything in its path. Total destruction was only second's away…seconds…'BUMMOOOOO' …..….Very close now….the end… 'BUMOOOOOO'…..silence. Silence…not a sound.

The switch had been turned off. Primrose looked around her surroundings as if awakening from a dream. Her mother and Peter hiding under the table, her father hanging onto his ears as if they would fly off at any second, she standing in the middle of the room, lost for words. Peter made the first move, clambering out from under his sanctuary. 'Not even a railway track within three miles,' he muttered to himself foolishly. Her mother got back onto two feet, eyeing the girl with both amazement and fear.

'Primrose, what have you done girl?'

None of the trio acknowledged Alec Green where he lay on the cold tiled floor. It would take him some time to realise that he was still in the land of the living. For the moment the stage belonged to his daughter. Dazed, unsure of the complete events of the last few minutes, Primrose was trying to rationalise the madness.

'I like it. I like it a lot,' said Peter, staring at his sister with newfound respect. Whatever action Primrose was involved in, he wanted a slice for himself. 'Wow! The train trick was out of this world.' Primrose knew she had some explaining to do. A lot of explaining to do in fact. As she wasn't aware of the magnitude of the last few hours she thought it better to pick through the maze in a methodical precise nature. To start at the beginning she would have to think of something nice.... the wind rustling through the trees that would do for starters. That always made her feel relaxed.....now....now she could remember. Ah, the beginning of the storm.

Chapter 6

Miss Sally rolled into headmaster Smyth's office feeling as though she had just been chipped out of a bunker onto the sixteenth green at Troon. Literally. Smyth had turned his spacious office into a replica putting green. Short grass colored carpet, hole in the middle of the floor complete with little red flag; Smyth's big oak desk overlooked the scene like a gallery. Miss Sally expected that at any moment a lark might fly by. Around the room cabinets and walls strained under an enormous amount of tin cups, silverware, knick-knacks and assorted golfing memorabilia. To add to the effect Chester Smyth sported a golfing customised haircut or more to the point….no hair. His bald pat was as shiny as anything found on a billiard table. Not another sports freak, thought Miss Sally. Perhaps Smyth would give her a warning by shouting…'FORE'…before knocking her through the window with his six iron.

'Sit down Miss Sally,' said the small, portly Smyth from behind his huge bunker, which in reality was just a desk, but it looked to Miss Sally like a bunker. When did you ever see a desk on the sixteenth at Troon for goodness sake?

With the morning sun streaming through the windows, only to be reflected off Smyth's dome, Miss Sally wished she had brought her shades. Decked out as he was in golfing attire, Miss Sally was in two minds to throw Chester Smyth one of his golfing caps from the nearby hat stand to relieve her retinas of the sunburn inflicted by the Smyth solar panel. Miss Sally slumped into a huge imposing armchair directly across the desk from the headmaster. She was glad, that from her new vantage point, she was shaded from the billiard ball reflection.

'How are you settling in?' asked Smyth, rolling a golf ball between his two out stretched hands on the desktop.

So weird were the surroundings that for all intents and purposes Miss Sally felt she was sitting on someone's lawn. She was in two minds to start with the weather forecast but decided to put humor to the back of her mind.

'I'm settling in fine, Mr Smyth,' she replied though at that moment wondering if Smyth watered his carpet.

'Good,' said Smyth, continuing to roll the ball to and fro across the table much to Miss Sally's annoyance. Miss Sally hated playing second fiddle to anyone, much less a stupid golf ball.

'Do help yourself to tea,' said Smyth, indicating a teapot on the desk. 'Just brewed.'

Miss Sally selected a cup from a tray, poured tea and milk, then against her usual habit, (for she hated anything too sweet), heaped liberal amounts of sugar into the cup. Anyone passing by would have taken Miss Sally for a tea white and fifteen kind of person, though Smyth didn't seem to notice. He was too engrossed in his game of hand ping-pong ball. Miss Sally took a sip. Uggghhh! The tea was so sweet that she screwed her eyeballs up and looked backwards into her brain. Composing herself, she launched into the next part of her plan. Putting her cup back on the saucer, she 'accidentally' spilt half the contents over the desktop.

'Jolly jumping golf balls!' shouted Smyth, swiping his ball away from the tidal wave cascading across his polished oak desk.

'Sorry,' protested Miss Sally, feigning surprise but pushing the film of tea with across the desktop in Smyth's direction. Smyth produced a duster to soak up the tea residue.

'It'll need another polishing now. Sugar really attacks the polish, you know. Makes the whole thing rather sticky.'

Not very good for rolling your ball, thought Miss Sally, though her manners prevented her from saying so.

'Oh! I'm so sorry Mr. Smyth. I only dropped in for a few seconds of your precious time.'

'Thank goodness for that,' said Smyth in a low voice but loud enough for Miss Sally to hear. Cleaning up the remainder of the mess he dropped the sodden duster into a waste paper bin then faced Miss Sally across the desktop. She gave a slight smile, knowing she had his complete attention. The next chip onto the green was hers.

'Shoot from the hip, Miss Sally. I'm sure I'm keeping you from something more important,' said Smyth, wishing to get rid of the troublesome female creature.

'It was on the matter of Mr. Knowles...' began Miss Sally before being interrupted.

'A very good teacher on the finer aspects of history and geography,' chirped Chester Smyth.

'I have no doubt about that,' replied Miss Sally, bouncing back. 'Though he's not so good on the finer aspects of rearing children.'

'I beg your pardon, Miss Sally,' ventured Smyth, missing the point entirely.

Miss Sally knew it would be utterly senseless beating around the bush so decided on an all out attack. 'You know the old one two,' she cried, putting on as snobby a public school boy tongue as she could manage. 'Off you go over the roof old chap. This will hurt me more than it'll hurt you. And if you're

extra, extra good…. I may just take you on the volley. Careful
not to scratch my boots now. There's a good fellow.
Whop…..wheeeeeee…..Oh! I nearly
forgot…..GERONIMOOOOOO.'

'Ok, ok, Miss Sally. Nuff said,' protested Smyth, holding up
his hands to signify surrender.

'Enough,' came back Miss Sally. 'Do you condone this type of
bullying behavior or are you just another spectator for the big
match at Twickers?'

'Not at all. There is a lot more to this than meets the eye. We
have to go back a bit in time to understand the makeup of
Knowles.'

'How far back…To the time of the Neanderthals, perhaps? The
man's a complete amoeba. No! No….that's an insult to an
amoeba,' said Miss Sally, referring to the simplest form of life,
a single cell creature. 'Can't you just sack the man from the
school? Send him to a coconut kicker's paradise on Easter
Island or somewhere? Anywhere that is far away from the
children.'

Smyth sighed, 'That seems like a very good option. The only
reason he remains here is because of the board.'

'Cheese board?' said Miss Sally, feigning stupidity.

'School board,' corrected Smyth.

'Then get them to give him the knuckle dancer, the heave ho.'

Smyth leaned forward a little, his head catching the sunlight once more. 'That's the whole point. They won't.'

'Why?'

'His rich aunt is a very influential member of the board who contributes varied amounts of funds toward the school. After Gavin's accident she kind of took him under her wing.'

'Then she wants to drop him from a very great height,' replied Miss Sally, making no attempt to conceal the hatred in her voice. 'A very great height.'

Chester Smyth retreated back into the shadows, a sure sign that he was in retreat from Miss Sally's onslaught. 'I'm afraid if that happens then the funds for the school will disappear as well. If it weren't for Mr. Knowles' accident then the school would never have found itself in this predicament. Poor fellow.'

'What poor unfortunate fellow are we talking about?' asked Miss Sally in complete bewilderment. Surely old Chester hadn't taken one too many on his old napper while out on the links. She knew the headmaster was going a bit senile, but sympathy for the Prince of Darkness was akin to putting your kids to bed with a man eating grizzly.

'Gavin Knowles of course, Miss Sally. If it wasn't for that accident.....wretched thing,' he shook his head. 'Then we wouldn't have found him in the teaching profession.'

'Perhaps he might have found his way into politics. Then he could have changed the law making the hoofing of children a compulsory pastime. Hey, old chap.... up and over Big Ben you go. Hey what!'

Miss Sally's sarcasm was lost on old Smyth. He was on a Gavin Knowles 'poor chap it'll be harder on me than you' trip. Smyth shook his head, 'It's a long story Miss Sally and not one I'm completely familiar with. You know how stories have the knack of turning into fairytales.'

'Yes I do,' said Miss Sally curtly. 'And if you must know, I do have time for a good tale. It may give me some ammunition in controlling Mr. Knowles excesses.'

'Do you fancy another cup of tea,' asked Chester glancing at her teacup.

'No thank you,' replied Miss Sally, wanting to get on with the story of Knowles' dark past.

'Well where to start.... now let me see. You have seen his deformed right hoofer?'

'Couldn't miss it, Mr. Smyth. It's like something a horse would jump over at a steeple chase.'

Smyth cracked a smile, 'Well put Miss Sally. A little bit of humor never did any harm. Anyway, Knowles was always a bit of a sportsman and as you can see,' he stopped to indicate his surrounding silverware with his hand. 'Mine is the gentler sport of golf.'

'Couldn't have guessed,' said Miss Sally waiting at any moment for a golfing party to cruise past on their way to the next green.

'Well, Knowles' sport was the old up and over. Don't know much about rugby myself, could never figure out why they had that misshapen ball for one. Silly thing…can't even roll properly. Never would see anything like that on the links.'

'Yes Mr. Smyth, I can see your point.'

'Where was I...?' asked Smyth, asking for a pointer as he had forgotten the plot.

'Knowles,' reminded Miss Sally.

'Yes of course, Knowles. How could I forget? I believe he was a scrum half or some such position but what he really excelled in, (and a lot of us have seen him in action), was as a place kicker. Conversions, penalties or whatever they call them. You know the old up and over the bar type of thing. Unique I'm told. Could place a ball on a sixpence.' Smyth paused to give a sigh. 'All came to a head when he came up against Toby Wilson.'

'Toby Wilson?' enquired Miss Sally as her curiosity factor kicked in.

'49 Schoolboys' Cup to be sure. Black Friars against St. Andrews. Everyone said the final would be a spiffer and it was. Knowles was in his element and was up for a bit of gamesmanship.'

Miss Sally fidgeted around in her humongous chair, 'Gamesmanship?'

'Oh, you know the kind of thing. Pulling the other players shirts out then sticking a handful of itching powder down the back of their y-fronts. Rake your studs along the back of an opponent's heel…. a finger in the eye. The old classic is laxative sweets given to the enemy before the start of the game, huh, huh, huh. Someone always falls for that.'

'No laugh for the other team,' said Miss Sally, somewhat disgusted at the lengths some people would go to in the name of sport. Diabolical.

'Sure can fritter your team away during the match,' continued Smyth, just managing to control his laughter. 'Heee heee hee. Instead of running for the ball they're running for the bog. Hee heee hee.'

Miss Sally drummed her knuckles on the desktop impatiently. She was tiring of Smyth's spoilt schoolboy toilet humor. Next thing he would be doing raspberries.

'Toby Wilson? Where does he fit in?'

Smyth composed himself managing to keep his laughter under control.

'Toby Wilson...now let me see...oh that Toby Wilson.'

Too long in the bunker thought Miss Sally. The old codger had lost his golf balls, now he was losing his marbles. Smyth snapped back to reality.

'Houdini Wilson, they called him. He was to trickery what Da Vinci was to art. He was an ace. Sneaky, dirty, tricky, innovative...all in the one package. Slick.'

Miss Sally was hanging on to the edge of the table in suspense.

'So?'

'So,' repeated Smyth, becoming distant once more.

'So....ah...yes. Wilson. 49 cup.' Smyth shook his head in some doubt. '48 maybe. Can't be sure now. Was it 48 or 49?'

It was all becoming too much for Miss Sally. '48 or 49. Get on with it man,' she shouted, unable to contain her excitement. Smyth's brain jumped out of neutral into gear once again.

'You're right, Miss Sally. 48 or 49...irrelevant to what happened. Though it was Twickers, mind you. Exciting game I was told. Everything was going down to the wall. Equally pegging in the dying minutes. 12 to 12 I believe. Very exciting, with Knowles playing a few aces through the game. The old itching powder down the trunk routine. Stink bomb lobbed into the scrum to split it up but for the grand finale he had thought up a real classic. Heeee heee hee.'

Off to cuckoo land again, thought Miss Sally. The man's attention span was little more than a few seconds. Without thinking Miss Sally cupped her hands over her mouth and roared, 'Fore!'
Well they were on a golf green after all, and anyway it seemed to get a reaction from the senile old golf cart.
'Yes, yes. A real classic. Stroke of genius, if you ask me. No one had thought of it before.'
'Well?'
'Yes…. the old whistle, Miss Sally. Threw the other team every time they had possession. The game would either slow up or Knowles' side would gain the ball while the Black Friar's stood around like statues. To be honest St Andrews were playing like a load of kindergarten kids with blindfolds on. Luckily Knowles produced the whistle in the second half to even things up. Anyway, to cut a long story short, even the referee was starting to get frustrated. He knew it had to have

been someone on the St Andrews team so he had them all lined up and searched. That was to change the course of the game.'

'Why?' asked Miss Sally, hoping that Smyth wouldn't lose track of the plot and have to start again at the beginning.

'Because Knowles had to sling the whistle and couldn't retrieve it. Things were looking better for the Black Friars but…' At that second Smyth paused and slammed his hand down on the desk like a clap of thunder. His face took on a most serious look.

'This is where fact and reality, myth and rumor converge.'

Miss Sally sat wide-eyed. Smyth's serious head changed once more to blankness.

'48 cup I think. Sure it was….hhmmm, maybe 49 when I think about it.'

Miss Sally wasn't about to let the cheese slip from the sandwich. Smyth needed more prompting to keep him on a roll.

'The rumor. The fact, reality, myth and rumor converging,' barked Miss Sally, trying to restrain herself from leaping across the desk and bouncing a golf club off Smyth's cranium to keep him in the land of the living.

'Well man?'

Smyth snapped out of his trance, 'Oh! Yes. Let me see. Yes….yes. Sometime in the scrum…or so they say. We can't be sure but it's presumed. How we don't know but all the evidence points to the scrum.'

'What points to the scrum, Mr. Smyth?'

Smyth made a cutting movement with two fingers of his right hand. 'Knowles got the snip.'

Miss Sally let out a low, 'Ohhhhh!' Her face contorted into a look of agony. She'd heard they could get rough on the rugger pitch… but the dreaded snip. 'Ohhh!' Jemima Sally's imagination was running away from her.

'Snipped his laces, girl. Pair of scissors or some such trickery,' snapped Smyth, trying to get the squeamish teacher to open her eyes.

'Oh! That snip,' said Miss Sally, opening her eyes and feeling rather foolish. At least she was back in control of her imagination once more.

'Devilish trick,' continued Smyth. No one realized the lace on Knowles right hoof was doctored until the penalty.'

'Penalty?'

'Twenty five yards out from Black Friar's goalmouth. St. Andrews still had a chance of clinching the game. Toby Wilson was so disgusted that his team had given away a penalty, that he booted the ball off the pitch. A boo went up from the crowd who saw this move as time wasting. There was only six minutes left of the game. Wilson dutifully tripped after the ball, reappearing back on the pitch a few seconds later. Ever the gentleman, and to show there was no bad feelings, he even placed the ball on the spot for Gavin Knowles. Knowles usually liked placing the ball himself but as he was so short for time he accepted the placing without a second thought.' Smyth stopped as his face took on the look of death. His voice became barely a whisper. 'If he had only checked the ball things....his life...so much could have turned out so different.'

Miss Sally's tongue went dry. She felt her heart beat so hard that it threatened to break through her ribcage. Goosebumps rose on her flesh, larger than the Himalayan mountain range. Smyth had become the storyteller extraordinaire, the focus of her attention. He was milking the story for all its worth. Miss Sally was trapped in a web of fact and reality, truth and rumor with her imagination on an away day to the moon.
'Why was that,' she asked in a whisper.
'Listen, all will be revealed. The whole stadium was in a deathly hush as Knowles lined up for the penalty and with his cry of 'Geronimo' he was off. The two pace kick was to be his final mistake. On his first stride his boot had already left his foot and was in midflight. He was committed.'

Miss Sally gave another low, 'Oohh!'

'Barefooted, Knowles made contact with the ball.
SCRUNCH!'

Miss Sally leapt three feet out of her chair as Chester Smyth kicked the bottom of his desk to create the proper sound effect. Miss Sally's heart had leapt into her mouth threatening to blow out her eardrums. Regaining her armchair, she clung on for dear life as Chester continued.

'The crunch could be heard throughout the stadium as bone and flesh met leather. The crowd had but a second to 'ahhh' before Knowles' bloodcurdling scream tore through the air, causing even the deafest of spectators' hair to stand on end. They say people from two miles away had feared it was the return of the blitz and they came running outdoors to the sound of the wailing human air raid siren. Horrible. Ugly.'

Miss Sally's face puckered up like a dried prune as her heart rate slowed to something like two hundred beats a minute. Smyth was in full swing, reveling in her discomfort. 'Sliced the ball, missing the bar entirely. Match over for St Andrews. With Knowles and the ball out of play, a second ball appeared and Black Friars seized the advantage. They ran the length of the pitch, tried and converted before St Andrews had time to pull their fingers from their ears.'

'The Prince of Darkness,' mumbled Miss Sally.

'Prince of Darkness. Don't recall if that feller was playing that day,' said Smyth, his mind rambling off once again. 'Black Friars or St Andrews.'

'A different match,' said Miss Sally. 'Silly me. Do you happen to know what happened to the ball?'

'Ripped right out of the stadium going like a missile,' said Smyth. He paused before continuing,

'Really strange that part of the story. It didn't end there. Really, really strange. Hhmmm.'

Miss Sally's heart dropped back into her ribcage. The Himalayan mountain range starting to recede. 'Why was that?' she whispered.

'Some kid found what appeared to be an egg about six months later in an allotment. Covered in moss it was, with five jagged gristly things growing from the egg. Thinking it was a dinosaur egg, the child handed it into the Natural History Museum.'

Smyth shook his head, 'You'll never guess what it was?'

Miss Sally didn't need two guesses, 'The ball.'

'That part was pretty evident when they removed the moss. I bet you can't guess what the other scaly things growing from the ball were?'

'No, I can't,' she replied, knowing Chester Smyth wouldn't be long in telling her. Smyth was back in the land of brothers Grimm. His eyes gleamed with a flicker of madness. 'The nails from poor old Knowles' pinkies.'

'What!' shouted Miss Sally, on the edge of her seat, before setting off on a trip to the Himalayas, chasing her imagination while her heart jumped into her mouth. She was once more in the realm of the paranormal.

'Yes, old Knowles hit the ball so hard that he left his nails embedded in the leather. They would never grow again. Hhhmmm, sure it was 48, maybe 49. Hhhhmmm I should ask him sometime but I think it may upset him somehow.'

'How could that happen?' gasped Miss Sally, slipping on the slopes of the mountain range where fact was stranger than fiction.

'You know how they say some things grow after a person has passed on?' said Smyth in his authoritative tone. 'You hear the stories that hair continues to grow, your nails too. Well not your nails, Miss Sally….huh uh…that the deceased carry on for a short time.'

'He really is the Prince of Darkness,' screamed Miss Sally as her hair stood on end.

'I'm sure that guy wasn't at the game. Never heard him mentioned before,' said Smyth to himself. 'I suppose he gets called POD for short. There were a few princes at St. Andrews now. Of Arabian descent, I believe. Don't ever recall a Darkness.'

Miss Sally was still trying to find her way through the maze of fact, reality, truth and rumor. Incredulous, to say the least, she found the whole event like something straight out of a fairytale. 'You mean his toenails were still growing six months later,' she gasped in wonderment.

'Oh! Yes, but they didn't grow much more than that. A strange phenomenon the people from the museum said. Once they realized that the nails belonged to Knowles they wanted to bring him in and do the old Froggy thing.

'Froggy thing?'

'Oh! You know dissection and that type of rubbish. All in the name of science of course. Much to their surprise, Knowles protested the length and breadth of the country. Lawyers, politicians, professors, all sorts were involved. They really wanted to give old Knowles the chop but finally they saw sense and threw him back on to the scrap heap. They say it was the most important event after that million year old dear they found in Ethiopia. Martha the modern woman, I believe they called her. Not a million years old of course…hhhheee heeee….heeee…. just dated around a million years since she was around.'

'How were her nails,' asked Miss Sally?

'Don't know my dear. All I know was that they tried to make a link between Gavin Knowles and some cave woman they found somewhere. I mean, just because a fellow loses some nails doesn't mean he's a cousin of the dinosaurs. Anyway, when the nails stopped growing the boffins took pity and handed Knowles back his ball.'

'He got it back?'

'Toe right,' replied Smyth. 'Ha ha ha. Get it? Toe right.'

Miss Sally gave the headmaster a stern look.

'Yes, yes. A bit silly I know,' he said glumly. 'But there was another strange part to the story.'

Miss Sally's heart was back in her ribcage. She had slipped down the mountain. She didn't feel ready for another shock, 'Surely not as strange as a set of pinkies growing from a ball?'

Smyth assumed the air of mystery once again. 'On close inspection the ball was found to be heavier…… a lot heavier than a normal ball. On even closer inspection it was found to be full of water. Ah ha!'

'Houdini?' Miss Sally said, just managing to contain herself.

'Perhaps he did the switch. Maybe the water found its way
there later, who knows?'

'I don't think so. When he kicked the ball off the pitch he must
have switched it. Then he conveniently placed it for Knowles,
knowing that his laces had already been chopped, Wow!'

'All suppositions,' interrupted Chester Smyth. 'Rumors,
nothing more than that. However, we do know it was the end of
Knowles' athletic career and his forthcoming commission in
the armed services. Couldn't find boots to fit him, poor chap.'
Chester gave a sigh, 'Became more twisted than ever after that.
Loves that ball like a girlfriend. Never lets it out of his sight.'

'Not the one he carries around in the holdall?'

'Yes, that'll be Bertha. Those two are bonded together by blood and bone. Can still see the gouges on her flanks. Now if that ball could talk we would hear a tale about the cup.'

'Well slap my face with a wet lettuce,' said Miss Sally glad that she had survived the ordeal of the 48-cup, or maybe the 49. Well 48 or 49.

'That Toby Wilson's sneakier than a fox with sneakers on called Sneaky. Whatever became of him?'

'They say he ended up somewhere in the armed services. What a team player to have on the side during a war. Eh what?'

'No doubt. The truth is somewhat stranger than fiction.' Smyth's face took on the look of an intelligent billiard ball, 'Yes. 48 or 49. I'm sure 48. No 49....'

Miss Sally made her excuses and left. She had endured enough surprises for the remainder of her days, but life in Red Kep was never far from the abnormal. There would be a few more surprises in store for the teacher.

Chapter 7

Primrose thought her happy thoughts and she was back in the field. She was there. The sparkles starting to fade away but one extra long sparkle fell into the patch right by her feet. If she felt strange before then what she was about to witness made strange seem very normal indeed. The whole vegetable field fizzled and crackled as if consumed by a fire but there was no heat. The power source was the falling sparkles, now glowing like the embers of a dying fire as they clung to the leaves and stems of the vegetation. Before her very eyes the vegetables started to shrink, withdraw into the ground, the exact opposite of growth, until finally there was nothing. The dying embers which had produced no heat faded into thin air. Then, IT happened. Primrose thought it was the extra long spark. Larger and more vibrant than the rest it had been dancing like a firefly as it fell near her feet. She fancied it was the sparkle but she couldn't be sure since her eyes were fixed on another part of the field. IT happened anyway. IT happened big time. Where all the other crops were consumed by the dancing fire flies, one brussels sprout stood alone. The falling sparkle combined all the atoms, molecules and elements which needed to come together at that crucial moment in time. This one sparkle kicked Mother Nature out of the window. Like a Chinese firecracker going off, the sprout grew as if fed by some magic growth elixir. As the leaves increased in size, deep within the sprout came a sound not unlike the burbling of a stream running down a mountainside, now and then reaching the crescendo of a cascading waterfall. As the bulk grew outwards, a low glow emitted from the sprouts inner leaves until POP! From the internals of the brussel there appeared to be something resembling a pair of huge luminous green eyes, which sat above a green, almost human mouth. When the eyes moved, for they were eyes after all, the evolutionary process was complete.

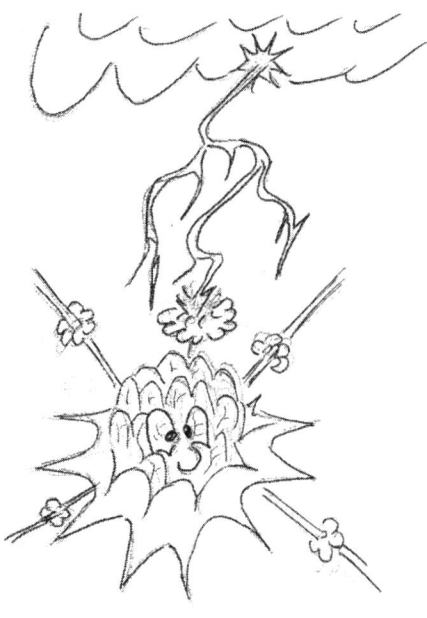

Whatever had been in the vicinity of the vegetable, whether bug, caterpillar, newt or ant, things had reached a fusion state in what Primrose would call the Big Bang. The phenomenon was the meeting of the known and the unknown. Stranger than anything in sci-fi this was spawned from the cosmos. The spark of life which was half-creature, half-plant. From between leafy lips, if you could call them lips, came the burble burble of something akin to communication.

If this was to be Primrose's sole purpose in life then she was ready. Her strange gift, acute uncanny hearing and the ability to mimic, had all increased 1000 fold since her encounter with the unworldly sparkles. Unafraid, she was prepared for the extraterrestrial encounter.

The Great, Incredible, Big Brussels Sprout felt weirdly out of place. Who was he? What was he doing? Why was he there? Was he even a he? Who was that other strange hairy green creature looking at him? Perhaps they were relations? 'Burbly gush gurly whoosh jurgly.'

Though a lot of the words, if you could call them that, sounded the same they were different because of their diverse tones. To Primrose, the sounds varied as the rise and fall of the surf on a beach. Primrose immediately sensed distress from the creature. He was afraid, as any creature would be in an alien environment. Before she realized what she was doing, Primrose had placed her hand on one of the brussel's shaking wet leaves. She didn't have to think about what to say. It just came naturally.

'Burbly blurbble walble gurgly urgly.'

Primrose found the sound of her own voice originating in a far off place. She did not feel any surprise. She accepted that she knew brussel speak. Beneath her hand she felt the leaf give a final shiver then stop.

'Blurp burlby gurgly goo goo,' came back the softly spoken reply as the giant brussels sprout blinked his eyes.

Definitely a male, thought Primrose. The brussel had a presence about itself that just cried male. He felt reassured, less frightened. Primrose, this weird hairy green creature that he had found would help him out in this strange world. Since he found his present circumstances odd, he tried to think back to happier times. He couldn't. There was nothing. The Great, Incredible, Big Brussels Sprout had no memory. He was without a past.

At that moment Primrose heard the sound of footfalls on soft ground, the labored breathing of an adult hurrying about their business. From her newly acquired super natural senses she knew, even at that distance, the person in question was her father on the way to visit his treasures. Boy was he in for a surprise. The sight of any ten-foot sprout would be enough to launch her father into brussels sprout heaven. A talking brussels sprout on the other hand was likely to put him in wooden box six feet under.

Primrose made a decision; she couldn't afford to let the brussel fall into the hands of her father. He would be used and abused to further her father's own ends in the green-fingered fraternity. No! She wouldn't let that happen. She talked softly to the giant brussels sprout, explaining that it was best that they move. He blinked his leafy-colored eyelids to show that he understood. He would go with her to a place of sanctuary where he would stay until Primrose returned for him later.

Primrose set off down the steep field then stopped, realizing that she was alone. Looking back into the darkness she could make out his huge silhouette against the skyline. He hadn't moved. He didn't know how to move. He had never moved before. Realizing that this was a problem, Primrose thought of a strategy.

'Upty glurgy urgly up,' coaxed Primrose into the darkness.

Listening to the girl, the giant brussels sprout began to rock from side to side by extracting and contracting his leaves. With the motion steadily increasing, he reached the point of no return and then began to roll.

'Glurryannn!' cried the giant brussels sprout as he set off at speed down the hill, passing Primrose in the process.

Primrose laughed heartily at the antics of the leafy bowling ball as he rolled, bounced and walloped his way down the incline.

'Got to learn sometime,' she said aloud, starting to follow the careering brussels sprout who had gathered more speed. She hoped he knew where to find his brakes before he reached something more solid. My! Things were exciting!

Primrose found the great brussels sprout turned upside down with his leaves caught up in a briar bush. Luckily his body was still on terra firma, though Primrose doubted if any bush could withhold several tons of sprouts without being flattened.

'Glory whoorly loorly goor!' he wailed, flailing his leaves at the same time.

'Silly boy,' thought Primrose, beginning to break off the branches.

With most of the branches away from his leaves the giant brussels sprout was able to use his weight to turn himself the right way around once more.

'Now stop being a silly boy and follow me,' said Primrose in brussel speaks.

Shaking his leaves again, the giant brussels sprout got his body moving once more. He was starting to enjoy this adventure. Primrose entered the thicket of woods while the giant brussels sprout brought up the rear. She emerged a few minutes later after reassuring the Great, Incredible, Big Brussels Sprout he would be quite safe there. Now the only thing left to do was to explain to her father where his field of vegetables had disappeared. Simple really.

'So that's what happened,' said Primrose, looking at her brother and mother. 'The whole truth and nothing but the truth.'
Primrose had told the truth but only regarding the part of the story she unveiled. She made no mention of a ten foot, talking brussels sprout roaming the countryside. For now the source of her supernatural powers was all that she would reveal. Her friend, the giant brussels sprout, could wait until a more opportune moment presented itself. If there would ever be an opportune moment to introduce a talking vegetable.
'Wow wee! That's some story, Primrose. Can you show us some more of those tricks?' said Peter, rubbing his hands

together gleefully. Gwen Green gave her son the look. She didn't have to say a word, Peter removed his smile. At that moment a groaning Alec Green dragged himself off the floor. His head felt like he had been at a practice session for the church bell ringers, his head replacing the bells. Through the banging in his head only one thought remained. Don't mess with Primrose. Of that he was sure.

Miss Sally glanced around her sparse surroundings, making sure everything was in its place. Stove was off, electric fire off, plugs out, plants watered. Quickly and methodically she went through her mental list. 'Hmm,' she mused, everything looked right. She gave a last cheery smile to the bright living room, slung her leather satchel over her shoulder and then picked up a rather heavy looking wooden box. A final reassuring glance and she was out of the door and on her way to her car.

She had managed to secure a years rent on the farmer's cottage and she was finally starting to knock it into shape as a home. She had planned a few trips down to her parent's home in London to pick up the last of her knick-knacks. Her rickety jalopy moved at a fair old lick along the bumpy lane, which led onto the main road. Miss Sally felt some contentment in the thought that she would introduce a different dimension into her pupils' usual monotonous routine. Excitement was needed.

Yes, this morning would be a little bit off the mark. The bumpy lane now behind her, she set sail towards Red Kep.

'Blurby uply blurbyy uppy lop,' said Primrose in greeting to her huge new friend. His eyes flickered open.

'Burp,' came the sound from his leafy lips. Primrose translated the burp into a rather more human yawn in response.

'Hey! You're making me feel tired too,' she called out in her own language and then broke into a laugh. The giant brussels sprout blinked his eyes, becoming accustomed to the sunlight then flapped his leaves much in the manner a bird would flap their wings. A few seconds later the world was in focus, his stretching exercises complete. The giant brussels sprout's eyes then jumped out to the end of their stems.

Primrose's partner was the centre of his attention. Long nosed, hairy, four legged and black; the creature had a swishing grass like contraption hanging from its hindquarters. All very unusual.

'Lurgy lurp surglly glurry up,' said Primrose as she tried to explain about Pippa the pony.

'Lurggy lurp up burp,' he replied, realizing that the pony had something other than grass swishing at its rear end. Primrose mentioned that it was in fact a tail. The great brussels sprout rolled nearer to Primrose and Pippa.

If the brussels sprout showed an interest in Pippa, then the pony showed an even greater interest in the brussel. Nestling closer to the brussel, Pippa gained a few more vital inches then …………..

'Aagghh!' came the murderous cry upon the still morning air. 'Much the same as human speak,' thought Primrose, pulling Pippa back. The scream didn't put Pippa off in the slightest. She happily gulped down the huge, leafy chunk of flesh she had detached from the brussel. Well what else was she supposed to do? Her nose was bombarded with the smell of food and her taste buds were bouncing off the back of her tonsils like a ten pin bowling ball. Well she did what came naturally. Ate. 'Crunch! Crunch! Crunch!' Lovely. 'Naughty girl,' scolded Primrose pointing a menacing finger at Pippa while holding the pony's bridles tight in her other hand. 'You can't be doing that.' Pippa took absolutely no notice as she devoured the remainder of the tasty tidbit. 'Hmm,' she thought, finishing off the remainder of the juicy morsel, another bit wouldn't go amiss. As Pippa moved forward the giant brussels sprout moved rearward. Primrose tightened her hold on the bridle.

'Blurgy gurgly floppy uppy,' roared the brussel as he cowered behind a tree, his leaves shivering with fear. Primrose translated the words into 'Why the heck are you trying to eat me.'

Nobody had told the giant brussels sprout that of all things he should expect to be eaten. Primrose thought it best to drop this subject at once. It could only lead to trouble for the giant brussels sprout to discover that he was at the lower end of a food chain, likely to be chased by a multitude of predators who would find him deliciously irresistible.

'Don't worry about it,' she said, in a very calming but not totally convincing voice. Primrose wasn't aware of any method to reassure a creature about to be eaten. She wouldn't much like it herself if she were in the middle of a tropical jungle surrounded by a group of saliva dribbling cannibals.

'There, there. Don't worry, we'll lightly broil you so you don't get de-hydrated and then we'll add lots of spices to give you a nice flavor. Don't worry; it'll all be tastefully done.'

The saying, 'we are having you over for dinner,' could literally mean just that.

'Am I safe,' asked the sprout as Primrose translated. 'Or will anything try to eat me out here?' he gurgled. Primrose showed she had a firm grip on Pippa.

'Don't worry Gibbs. It'll be alright,' said Primrose in brussel speak.

'Gibbs,' repeated the confused brussel. What or who was a Gibbs?

'Gibbs,' Instead of calling you Great, Incredible, Big Brussels Sprout, I just take the first letters of each word and call you Gibbs.

'What's a brussels sprout?' asked the brussel, shaking his leaves in horror as Pippa rolled her tongue around her lips as she looked hungrily in his direction.

'You are,' answered Primrose. 'Gibbs, the brussels sprout.'

'Oh am I? What are brussels supposed to do then?'

Primrose glanced at her wristwatch, feigning surprise.

'Oh my, is that the time! I really must rush or I'll be late for school. I can tell you all about that later.'

'Are you taking that creature with you?' asked Gibbs, concerned for his safety.

'Don't you worry about Pippa. She'll be locked up out of your way. So you be sure to stay here until I get back.'

'Can't I go for a roll?' he asked.

'No, No, No,' implored Primrose.

'Why?' asked the giant brussels sprout.

'Because you're strange,' she said in brussel speak.

'Strange?' came back the reply.

'People haven't seen anything like you. They'll chase you, pursue you. You'll be victimized,' replied Primrose in a series of glory uboorgly urdlys.

'What's victimized?'

'Something similar to what Pippa just did to you,' answered Primrose, holding onto the pony who continued looking at the brussels sprout with hunger in her eyes.

'Eat me you mean?' was the fearful reply from the brussel.

'No, nothing like that,' insisted Primrose. 'It's much better for you to stay here until I can show you around. Show you the ropes if you get my drift.'

'Ropes?'

'Forget it. I'll show you later,' said Primrose pulling a very reluctant pony after her.

The giant brussel sprout made a move as if to follow. Primrose wasn't in the mood for more explanations. She really had to get to school.

'Stay there or risk being eaten,' barked Primrose, her face set as hard as stone. She hated using bullying tactics but hoped Gibbs would pay heed to the threat for his own welfare.

'Glurrgg uppll joollyy,' which roughly translated meant 'what a horrible creature.'

The giant brussel reluctantly retreated into the safety of the woods. Primrose made off to secure Pippa for the day before beating a hasty skip to school.

The pupils shifted uneasily in their seats anticipating the treat promised to them by Miss Sally. All that morning they all had imagined what lay inside the polished engraved wooden box. To a young wondering mind the box contained anything from a simple chocolate biscuit to diamonds and gold. What delights did Miss Sally have in her Pandora's Box?

'Very well children. You've behaved splendidly today,' said Miss Sally, looking over the top of her glasses. All eyes were on the teacher as she stood beside the prized box. Miss Sally undid the latch, holding down the lid of the box.

'I'm sure everyone has seen one of these at some time.'

The pupils weren't sure on that score. The delicately engraved box confused onlookers with figures of dancing nymphs, sprites and animals in an enchanted landscape. The customized box, of some Asian extraction, sucked the young observers into its mystery.

As necks craned forward in a giraffe-like fashion, Miss Sally threw back the lid and withdrew... a black snakelike creature…which in a few seconds they recognized as an electrical lead.

'It's a record player,' called out Bert Eccles from his vantage point next to Miss Sally's desk.

Reassured that Bert was, in fact, correct; the pupils pulled their necks back in and regained their seats. Miss Sally smiled as she plugged the lead into a socket.

'No, not exactly a record player, Bert. This is a phonograph,' said Miss Sally, rummaging in her satchel for a few other goodies.

'Bah, that's not very exciting,' came the call of a young voice from somewhere at the rear of the class.

Miss Sally continued to smile, 'Don't be so silly. This is something exciting. Just let your imaginations do the talking.'

Miss Sally removed a LP disc from a cardboard sleeve and delicately gave the surface a clean with a handkerchief to make sure no dust was on it.

'Can that old antique go, Miss?' said the immaculately pressed and creased Andrew Archibald.

'His father must have forgotten to starch his lips,' thought Miss Sally. 'Cheeky little rascal.' Anyway she knew a means to make all the sour pusses even more sourly, 'Maybe you would all like to do another lesson of maths, or those that don't want to be part of this lesson could join Mr. Knowles' class for a spell.'

A silence descended on the ensemble.

'Well, answer?' said Miss Sally in as gruff a voice as she could.

'No, Miss,' came the unanimous reply.

Miss Sally took a batch of pamphlets from her desk then dropped the papers along the front row of pupils.

'Take one each then pass the rest on please.'

She watched as the pupils received their pamphlets before returning to her seat. She carefully set the disc on the revolving turntable and knocked over the arm to begin the play.

'Now let your imagination run wild. Don't just listen. Use all of your senses. Here it comes.'

As the first chorus struck, Miss Sally relaxed back in her chair. The soothing tones of the music made her close her eyes. Though the phonograph looked ancient its sounds were far from creaky. The phonograph was a present from her Aunt Hetty who had returned a few years earlier from a round the world jaunt. She had acquired the phonograph from a bazaar in Istanbul and brought it especially for her favorite niece. Aunt Hetty, who never married, had spent her adult years as a concert pianist until the onslaught of rheumatism put paid to her career. She rather hoped Jemima would follow in her footsteps since she possessed an aptitude for music. It was not to be however. Her brother, Jemima's father, thought that money could be better spent than putting his daughter through musical college. Being an industrial manager, Robert Sally, thought the arts were airy-fairy, a complete waste of time. Protestation from Jemima's sisters and her mother fell on deaf ears. A proper job was needed. With her sisters married off to rich husbands, which suited her father, Jemima fell into the next best thing. Teaching. At least it paid a wage and got her away from her father's watchful gaze. Though life went on, her love for music was still there. An experience she now wished to share with her pupils. And sharing it she was as her record blared out a compilation of Gilbert and Sullivan's hits with tracks from the Mikado, the Gondoliers, HMS Pinafore and the Pirates of Penzance. Something the youngsters could relate to that wasn't too heavy on the operatic theme.

It happened on the Mikado track, 'The sun whose rays are all ablaze,' which was very near to the end of the record. Miss Sally's students had been excellent throughout; daydreaming, doodling or even listening to the music. Then the first signs surfaced that everything wasn't as it should be. Miss Sally wasn't aware that there was a scratch on the record's surface.

If she had second thoughts on the matter then she wouldn't have played the disc on the first place. She heard a slight glitch in the record and upon opening her eyes she saw the arm retracting back into its rest. The music stopped for the record was no longer playing but the singing continued. The pamphlets Miss Sally had passed out earlier contained all the words to the music so her pupils could follow the individual tracks. However the singing wasn't the amateurish attempt of some school kid. This was the Mikado singer ....without the music.

Miss Sally took a double check on the phonograph. Nothing. It had stopped. If she didn't believe her eyes ...... then she surely didn't believe her ears. Immediately she felt the hairs rise on the back of her neck. Something uncanny was happening. A supernatural force was at work.

'I MEAN TO RULE THE EARTH AS HE THE SKY. WE REALLY KNOWWWWWW OUR WORTH THE SUN AND I I I I I I I I..........'

Miss Sally's eyes flitted from the phonograph to her class. Still the song blared out. The Mikado singer singing without her backing music, somehow the singer's voice had thrown the bonds and confinements of the phonograph. Gone into another dimension. Eerie. Unearthly. It couldn't be somewhere in the room?

If Miss Sally was looking for an answer then she wasn't alone. Already children in the class were searching for the origin of the ghostly voice. All eyes bar one pair, moved as if attached to one head. When they all faced, bar one, in the same direction then the mystery was answered. Or was it? There, at the rear of the class with her head thrown rearward, the soprano's tonsils floated like a piano key as she picked notes out of mid air.

'AH PRAY MAKE NO MISTAKE WE ARE NOT SHYYYYY. WE'RE VERY WIDE AWAKEEE THE MOON AND I I I I I I I I I I I I I I I I I I I I I I I.'

She seemed to hold the last note forever and a day. 'Well tickle me under the armpit with a hedgehog,' thought Miss Sally in total amazement. The words were so surreal. Yes there was no mistake. No mistaking .... the undeniable Primrose Green. Miss Sally wouldn't have believed it if she were not witness to the phenomenon. Though there was ample space in Primrose's thatch to hide an entire orchestra, there had been no trickery, no ventriloquism, and no outside interference. Of that Miss Sally was certain. The girl was undoubtedly the singer.

Upon dropping her head, Primrose was greeted by row after row of faces showing utter amazement. Eyes hung out of their sockets on stalks. Mouths hung open like Venus flycatchers. The only sound a ghostly, deathly silence. 'So that was the girls secret,' thought Miss Sally, trying to regain her senses. She was a gem in a bucketful of mud, a swan in a throng of turkeys, a diva of the highest note. The voice magnifico. Miss Sally's natural reaction was to clap. Slowly at first, the others joined in. The ice broken, Primrose's classmates wouldn't be held back. They let off an almighty appreciative roar which threatened to lift the rafters off the roof. Blushing ever so slightly, Primrose smiled. It was the first time she had known adulation. Though the feeling was strange, somehow she felt warm inside. Contented.

'That's enough, children. We don't want Primrose to get carried away now do we?' shouted Miss Sally above the noise. The pupil's applause dropped off as they turned to face the front of the class. At that moment the school bell rang signaling the end of the school day. Miss Sally was glad of the break.
'Right off you go then. See you all tomorrow.'
The children didn't need to be told to leave. The school bell always emptied seats quicker than a fire in a fire works factory. They were off.

'Oh don't rush away Primrose,' said Miss Sally as she spied the girl trying to tiptoe lightly past her desk.

'Perhaps you could help me with a few things?'

Caught short, Primrose approached the teacher nervously, 'What would you like me to do?'

'Oh, just help me tidy up my things,' answered Miss Sally.

No harm in that, thought Primrose, though she waited for the inevitable embarrassing questions on her performance. Oh if only the record hadn't gone off, then nobody would have discovered her secret.

'Oh, Miss, I'm not in a rush anyway,' said Primrose, dropping her bag on the floor to help Miss Sally pack her records into her satchel.

'You like music I can see,' ventured Miss Sally choosing her words carefully.

'Yes, well I mean…..no. I ………. no… I mean yes.'

'You do?'

'I do but I never do, if you know what I mean,' broke off Primrose.

No, Miss Sally didn't know. She was more confused than ever, 'I think I'm getting you. You do but you don't. Is that correct?'

Primrose made a grimace, 'I mean I love music but I never listen to it…you know'

'You mean never, ever?'

'Yes,' Primrose replied.

Miss Sally was more taken aback than before. Must be spraying her hair with weed killer or some substance. The child was losing the plot. How could she sing like a lark and never listen to music. No, she was holding something back.

'You mean you've never played an instrument? Sung songs round the old campfire? Screamed football chants on a Saturday afternoon?'

Primrose's face remained blank. Miss Sally closed down the lid of her phonograph.

'No nothing like that. Ever.'

Miss Sally believed Primrose but to have some understanding of the situation she thought it better to subject the girl to a little test.

'Could you please give me your deepest note Primrose?'

Miss Sally could see Primrose turn a deeper shade of green. Embarrassment was paying her a visit.

'Oh, it's not that important. I thought you might be able to help me out with a scientific experiment that's all.'

'Scientific experiment?' repeated Primrose as she felt her face return to its normal hue of green.

'No, don't you worry, girl. I'm sure I can find someone else to help,' said Miss Sally about to throw her satchel over her shoulder.

Primrose touched her teacher's arm lightly, 'If it's for a scientific purpose I would like to help, Miss.'

Miss Sally placed her satchel on the desktop, 'Ok, you've talked me into letting you help, Primrose.' said Miss Sally, smiling.

'What's the experiment?' asked Primrose with a newfound gleam in her eye.

'Ah voice range,' said Miss Sally, hesitating as she tried to think of something scientific to say. 'You know the pitch of the voice is controlled by air passing over the vocal chords here,' she broke off, pointing at her throat with a finger.

'Well I was just wondering how deep you could go. Myself I can go like this BOOOOOOOOOORRRRRRHH.'

Primrose gave a laugh, before clamping her hand over her mouth to stop giggling.

'Yes, that's about as deep as I can go. Why don't you give it a try, Primrose? Go on,' encouraged Miss Sally.

Primrose cleared her throat as she composed herself 'BOOOOORROHHHHHHHHHH.'

Miss Sally felt the walls shaking as the sound reverberated off them. The rumble felt as if an earthquake was about to happen. Any deeper in pitch and the two of them would find themselves in Australia. Miss Sally held up her hand to show she had heard enough. The noise would have put any baritone or bass in the shade. Miss Sally was amazed but managed to keep her composure.

'How was that,' enquired Primrose in her normal feminine voice.

'Rather good,' said Miss Sally. 'I wonder what you're like at the top end of the scale.'

'Would you like me to try one?' asked Primrose, arching her neck forward as she prepared to saturate her vocal chords.

'Yes go ahead. Give us one.'

Primrose's throat opened and out came the voice of a lark. Seconds later the pitch increased to that of a shrill whistle, in a few more seconds the sound became that of a jet engine. The windows started to rattle.

'Stop,' screamed Miss Sally as loud as she could, but she was drowned out by Primrose's shrill voice. Miss Sally grabbed Primrose by the arm and gave her a shake before she hit the crescendo, or more to the point, before the crescendo hit them. Primrose stopped abruptly. The windows stopped rattling as Miss Sally thanked her lucky stars that she wasn't permanently deafened.

The girl was a powerhouse of untold vocal strength, ranging from the bellow of a water buffalo to the screech of a scalded cat. And all this without any training. Absolutely incredible. Miss Sally had never come across anything like it in her life.

'Is this the secret you were going to tell me about, Primrose?'

Primrose shook her head causing her resident flower population to gyrate to the beat.

'Not really Miss.'

'You mean such a voice and you didn't think to tell me about it?'

'It's not just the voice Miss ....'

Miss Sally's eyes widened, 'There's something more?'

'No. I mean ... well it's hard to explain.'

Well if it was hard for Primrose to explain, it was even harder for Miss Sally to comprehend. Since her arrival in Red Kep the teacher's life had been one long line of surprises. Now there was another one to add to the list.

'Go ahead Primrose, don't be shy.'

Primrose gave a sigh of relief, 'I'm able to detect sounds better than most people. It's my hearing, you see,' began Primrose, feeling more relaxed in Miss Sally's company. 'It's so very, very... What would you call it?'

'Acute?' cut in Miss Sally.

'Yes, that's it, acute, yes.'

'Why is that?'

'Because I'm outdoors so much alone and all I have to listen to is....... sound.'

'You mean to say that you can hear something I can't?'

'I know I can hear something. You can probably hear it too but you don't know you can,' explained Primrose, putting a finger to her lips, 'Sshhhh and listen.'

Miss Sally listened. She listened ever so intently but could hear absolutely nothing. She shook her head in dismay.

'Listen,' hissed Primrose, 'one more try.' Miss Sally held her breath as she concentrated. Her face starting to go blue with oxygen starvation, she threatened to burst.

'There, did you hear that?' called out Primrose.

'NO,' gasped Miss Sally, steadying herself on the side of the desk as she started to see stars.

'You're concentrating too hard. Look.'

Primrose lifted a nearby plant pot to reveal a spider, which promptly set off at high speed to find another cubbyhole.

'They scurry, you know,' said Primrose putting down the plant pot.

'How ....PANT...could you...PUFF....hear him,' gasped Miss Sally, trying to regulate her breathing.

'I told you I have an ear for it. Been around creatures all my days. I know every sound, every squeak that they make.'

Miss Sally pushed her glasses back on her slender nose. The girl never ceased to amaze her. She had the voice of an angel and the ears of a Doberman pincher with a hearing aid. What talent.

'Your voice?' asked Miss Sally, her breath returning.

'Voice?' came back Primrose, not understanding what her teacher meant.

'How did you develop your voice without any proper training?'

'Oh that was very easy.'

'How did you develop that incredible range? I've never heard a voice like it.'

'It didn't take very long.'

'A few years, months maybe?'

'Nothing like that,' said Primrose timidly.

'How long?' asked Miss Sally. At that second a fly flew into the room through an open window.

'Oh let me see ... just the other night.'

Miss Sally gasped in astonishment as the housefly was flying past. The fly was sucked in by the vortex of forces into the throat of the schoolteacher. Miss Sally didn't appreciate the gastronomic delight, so she dipped her coughing and spluttering face into a waste paper basket. The coughing and spluttering continued until she managed to regurgitate the bedraggled, now defunct creature into the bottom of the basket.

'Poor critter,' said Primrose. 'Didn't even know what hit him. Still, better than sudden death at the hands of our friend the spider.'

Miss Sally dropped the bin back on the floor and grasped the desk as she tried to fight the spasms in her larynx. At last she got her gag reflex under control

'You mean … you mean to tell me, Primrose, you only learned a day ago?'

Primrose smiled, thinking back to her baptism of fire in the vegetable patch, 'It sort of happened kind of sudden. I wasn't really trying but it happened and that was it.

Miss Sally straightened up, regaining her dignity after her encounter with the fly.

'Could you be so kind as to tell me how this happened?'

Primrose thought her teacher had enough surprises for one day. If she were to tell Miss Sally any part of the story it would have to be the abbreviated version. The Mark 1 tale wasn't too far-fetched and contained a sprinkling of the paranormal.

'Well when I was out on the farm the other night....'

'Not during the dreadful storm?' interrupted Jemima Sally.

'Look Miss Sally, would you like to hear my story or not?'

Miss Sally knew she was out of order. Better not to put the shutters up between the two of them by asking nosey questions.

'Carry on Primrose. I am a brick wall, silent.'

Primrose nodded in agreement, 'Well it went something like this ....'

Chapter 8

Primrose tethered Pippa to a post before setting off to find her very unusual friend. She had related to Miss Sally the story of her newfound powers, opting to leave out any mention of a ten-foot talking brussels sprout. She didn't want to delve into the realms of what adults would see as comic book fiction. A walking, talking brussels sprout indeed. They would say she was eating so many greens that she was in danger of turning into a sprout herself. The facts would have to remain concealed for the meantime.

Primrose neared the woods, calling out 'Gibbs' as she approached. No sign of the brussels sprout. She entered the small thicket of trees calling out his name as she walked. Nothing. He wasn't to be seen and being so large, there was no way Gibbs could possibly hide from her. No, he wasn't there. Primrose found her way back to the woods entrance. She didn't know what to do next. A definite missing brussel alert was called for. What would she do? Go to the police telling them she had lost a ten-foot brussels sprout and if they should come across him he answered to the name of Gibbs. Yes officer, Gibbs spelt G I B B S.

'Has he not got a second name?' the officer would ask.

'Hamm,' mused Primrose, seeing difficulties ahead.

Where had the blighter gone, when she had expressly told him not to leave!

Primrose was trying to formulate a plan when she picked up the first glimmer of hope. She could hear the swish of a shard of grass; the flattening of a strand, sounds equating to motion. Gibbs was on the move. Primrose turned away from the wood looking towards the north meadowlands. With her super sensitive hearing she could tell that the Great, Incredible, Big Brussels Sprout was on the go without seeing him. She was proven correct when a few seconds later Gibbs came rolling over a hill into plain view. Cruising down the hill at speed, Gibbs only had to negotiate a high hedge separating himself from Primrose. His roll, combined with a flap of his leaves, created enough bounce to carry him over the obstacle.

Primrose was so impressed that she clapped and 'Yoh howed!'

Gibbs pulled out his leaves coming to a standstill.

'Girgly up sinly gurlgy ------------,' 'What's up then sport?' he asked.

Primrose looked at the half-creature, half-vegetable and could see that he was not his normal self. When did several tons of vegetable ever resemble normal, she asked herself.

'You're looking a bit down.' said Primrose in his language, daring to touch one of the brussel's wilting leaves. 'A drop of water should freshen you up.'

'I've had a splash in a pool nearby,' he replied.

'You're getting around a bit,' said Primrose, continuing to pick up more signs of decimation on the brussel's foliage.

'I gotta do what a Gibbs gotta do.'

'Did you have anything to eat?'

'What does a brussels sprout eat?' asked Gibbs.

Good question thought Primrose. Gibbs was no sprout head. He had a mouth but Primrose hadn't the foggiest what a moving, breathing vegetable should have to sustain his body.

'I don't know. I thought water might be enough.'

'I don't feel hungry. Maybe I could develop a taste for that four legged cabbage cruncher you hang out with.'

Primrose was baffled. She screwed her face up.

'Cabbage cruncher?' she asked.

'Your friend. That hairy smelly creature.'

'Oh you mean Pippa?'

'The cabbage cruncher.'

Primrose gave a hearty laugh, 'Very funny Gibbs, but you're not a cabbage, you're a sprout.'

Gibbs mouth turned into a snarl at the very thought of Pippa, 'Doesn't seem to worry her. How would that four legged defoliant cum manure spreader like it if I took a piece out of her?'

'Not a lot. I'm sure.'

'Not at all, I bet. I may just try one of her legs for size the next time we meet.'

Primrose feared for Gibbs' safety. Recently he had started to become more inquisitive and liked to know what was happening around him. She would return later after school when she could spend more time with him.

'How many times do I have to tell you about wondering off on your own? People aren't used to seeing giant brussels sprouts hopping all over the place.'

After saying the words Primrose felt rather stupid. Would people ever get used to seeing a ten-foot brussels sprout jumping all over the place?

Gibbs replied in brussel speak, 'There are a few strange creatures out there I'm not sure of either. They scare the living chlorophyll out of me.'

Primrose smiled. Gibbs' vocabulary was improving greatly thanks to his nosiness and constant interrogation of Primrose for answers.

'All the more reason for you to stay close to home. I'll call again in the afternoon.'

'Oh ok,' said Gibbs. 'I'm feeling a bit tired after that splash I had earlier. I may have a nap.'

'Surgly,' said Primrose for bye.

Bye came back the reply from Gibbs as Primrose set off on her travels.

Primrose was definitely worried about Gibbs. She could see that his leaves were beginning to wither and die. Water wasn't enough to nourish him but she didn't know how to feed a vegetable without any roots. Perhaps the only solution would be to put him in a freezer. No, that would never do. How would he breathe? She would have to think of another solution but ...... yesterday.

The morning was bright with a hint of dew on the ground. A very pleasant morning, thought Miss Sally. But what of the rest of the day? She wondered what that would be like. Miss Sally watched her pupils embark onto their bus.

'Careful now, Sarah Jane,' said Miss Sally to Sarah Jane Lewis who was so busy looking around her that she bumped into the bus steps with her shins. 'No crying now, it wasn't that bad.'

Sarah Jane gave a painful smile, bit her lip and boarded the bus. Miss Sally knew that day outings were always a trying time.

From her own schooldays she was aware that mischief and trouble were never too far from adventuresome children.

'I'm watching you lads,' reminded Miss Sally to Bert Eccles and his pal Sam Rea who looked like they were ready for a day of devilment.

'Morning Miss,' uttered the duo, racing aboard the bus looking for a seat.

'Tally Ho, old girl!' came the booming voice from across the car park.

Miss Sally didn't have to look in the direction of the other bus to know whom the voice belonged to but out of politeness she did so. Sure enough, it was the pinheaded knuckle dragger Mr. Knowles, throwing on the last of his prisoners.

'Be there or be square,' he roared, hanging out of the bus door with his surf board of a foot planing in the wind as the bus moved off.

'Twit,' called out Miss Sally to the retreating form of Knowles.

Jemima Sally had been unlucky enough to be paired with Knowles' class for the excursion to the local airbase, but that was the way of the world. Sometimes you had to take the rough with the smooth. Anyway, Knowles was sure to be on his best behavior as the air force people sought to build bridges with the local community. The top-secret flight squadron, so top-secret in fact, that it was only referred to as X flight, hoped to keep on the right side of their neighbors by keeping their noisy, low flying sorties to a minimum. Public relation exercises always seemed to help.

Miss Sally spied Primrose Green as the straggler in her own little group.

'Morning Primrose.'

In her own little world, thought Miss Sally, and what a totally amazing world that was turning out to be.

'Morning Miss,' mumbled Primrose, boarding the bus.

Definitely not a morning person, thought Miss Sally, boarding the bus herself. Miss Sally looked down the aisle of the bus and had a quick head count. Certain that all the little blighters were there, she gave the bus driver the thumbs up and off they rattled.

Alec Green found his way to Kale Knarsnock's shop on his quest for the return of his lost vegetables. With the upcoming flower and veg show now a mere few days off, his vegetable epitaph would read, 'Alec Green nothing to field.' He had been literally stripped bare in the face of the horticultural and farming communities. How embarrassing, especially being nobbled right before the main event of year. The police had drawn a blank on any clues leading to the recovery of his beauties so his next port of call was to Knarsnock. The man was always a wealth of information on any subject.

Knarsnock was his usual shifty self in his lair of perpetual darkness. Alec Green thought the Norwegian had thrown his lot in with daylight to become a creature of the night. Nothing wrong with that, he often used the technique himself to get his bulbs to sprout before moving them outdoors.

'Am doing for you what?' asked Knarsnock, his green cat-like eyes now bloodshot and looking more like an AA road map than those of a human.

Alec Green propped his elbows up on Knarsnock's countertop, 'A little notice in your local rag would be of some help.'

'I can do, yes. For what?'

Green felt the bile rise in his throat. Talking about the theft of his vegetables was still a touchy subject.

'Concerning the diabolical theft of my greens. Total decimation. Not a lettuce leaf left. Years of work gone. Should be laws passed through parliament for that type of thing. Hang the blighters. Vote in the green party, they would never stand for that type of terrorism. Never.'

'Something you have lost?' asked Knarsnock, barely able to keep his eyelids open.

A beta-carotene fix, thought Green. Only ever found in the right quantities in carrots. That should do the trick, or failing that a couple of matchsticks.

'Anyway Mr. Knarsnock, I have had my sprouts nicked.'

'Sproutnik!' exclaimed Knarsnock, his road maps expanding to a larger size.

'Sproutnik, man! My whole patch is gone!' shouted Green, trying to get his point through to the Norwegian.

'Patch gone?'

'All gone. My sprouts took the worst hammering. Totaled.'

Totaled?' came back Knarsnock.

Green slammed his fist down on the wooden counter top.

'Don't keep repeating what I say man. Have you got the message or what?'

'Or what,' repeated Knarsnock, nodding his head in agreement.

'There you go again, Knarsnock. Have you got my drift yet?'

'Sproutnik totaled or what?' answered Knarsnock.

'You've hit the nail on the head,' said Green, changing his tone. 'Now what I want you to do is put an advertisement in your rag offering a reward for the return of my greens or any information leading to their recovery. Know what I mean?'

'Yes indidee,' replied Knarsnock, using his new phrase that he had just picked up off a western movie that he had seen.

'Stick it in as soon as you can, man. Don't specify any sum for the reward,' said Green, formulating a plan to give as little as possible as a reward. Tight being his middle name, Green reckoned a year's supply of pig manure would be bonus enough. He couldn't foresee too many takers for a spot of the old smelly trotter's seconds.

'Done it is,' said Knarsnock, anxious to get back to his nocturnal activities.

Green said, 'Alright, man,' but wondered at the same time if things would indeed be alright.

Knarsnock's bloomers were legendary. No, not his skimpies, but rather his editorial cock-ups. To start with, there was the time Granny Knot was doing her rounds collecting raspberries for her preserves. As fate would have it the local village bus blew a tire while rounding a blind corner. The bus careering towards her at speed, Granny Knot and her pram were lucky to be brushed aside to crash through a soft bush. Though the bus landed on its side, thankfully no one was injured. The only casualty for the entire episode was the damage to Granny Knot's raspberries. If Granny Knot wasn't physically hurt, then her pride most certainly took a bashing when Knarsnock's paper appeared with the headline ......'BUS CRUSHED BY MRS KNOT'S RASPBERRIES.' In reality the heading should have read, 'MRS KNOT'S RASPBERRIES CRUSHED BY BUS.' Then there was the report of Mr. Green's high altitude barbecue burner, which grabbed the headlines as 'UNKNOWN WHY VILLAGERS ENJOYED TOASTED GOOSE FOLLOWED BY PIG MANURE SOURCE.' With a few careful alterations to the words a more pleasing headline should have read ....'VILLAGERS ENJOY TOASTED GOOSE. SOURCE OF THE FOLLOWING PIG MANURE UNKNOWN.' If that wasn't enough damage done to the local hotel and catering trade, then to cap it all Knarsnock was asked to write a short article for visiting tourists. Trying to find a descriptive term for Red Kep he came across a perfect example in an English medical journal. This would eventually end up as 'RED KEP: A GREAT AND ANGRY PIMPLE RISING FROM THE BACKSIDE OF THE LOCAL COMMUNITY.' Nobody could hazard a guess what the headline should really have read but thought things best left to one's own imagination. Knarsnock's understanding of English left a lot to be desired, so much so in fact, that the locals thought of changing the name of the paper from the Red Kep Recorder to the more apt Red Kep Decoder. Still, for all his eccentricities, the Old Norwegian certainly brought a smile to most of his readers' faces.

'Right I'm off,' said Alec Green, about to go through the door. 'You really could do with a spot of dusting in here. Ideal environment for growing mushrooms you know.'
Knarsnock pulled back his mouth in a smile. With the faint speck of light flooding through the door, Knarsnock's usually yellow teeth appeared to be stained red. Green had to take a second gawk.
'Eating too much of that red meat, Mr Knarsnock. You really should try some of my sprouts you know.'
'Sprouts?' repeated Knarsnock.

'Yes, you're right old man, sprouts. Them dirty, thieving scoundrels. It's enough to make my blood boil.'

Alec Green was still talking when he realized he was standing on the street alone. With his blood still on the boil, he stomped off in the direction of the police station to see if there were any further developments on his vegetable heist. From behind Knarsnock's door, a bolt could be heard locking into place. The faintest hint of a demented laugh signaled that the Norwegian was once more closed to business.

Chapter 9

The buses parked up inside Red Kep Royal Air force base. Miss Sally wasn't in the slightest bit looking forward to spending the day with Gavin Knowles but presumed at least that his behavior would be exemplary. Alighting from their transport, the two classes lined up behind their respective teachers. A slim, clean-shaven officer in his air force blue uniform stepped out from the adjacent movements office.

'Hello. I'm Wing Commander Flatly. At your service,' he said, shaking the hands of the two teachers. 'I hope to show you around our establishment and give you an idea what we're about.'

Miss Sally had to bite her lower lip to refrain from giggling. The Wing Commander talked like he was chewing on an extra large gobstopper. Definitely from the toffee nosed gobstopping debating society, she thought to herself. At that second a sleek, slippery super fast jet roared over the assembled group and headed skywards.

'It's the super duper zillion miles per hour secret X flight jet,' screamed an excited Bert Eccles to his pal.

Wing Commander Flatly couldn't help but overhear the remark., 'I heard that young fellow. Loose lips sink ships and all that hoo hah.'

'Or for that matter blabbering bumpkins lead to junkyard jets,' said Knowles, fixing the boys with a stare as the Prince of Darkness tapped out a nervous rhythm on the tarmac. Could be several conversions coming up, thought Miss Sally, watching the nervous twitch of the POD. Bert Eccles had a set of ears that fell nicely to the hand. Perfect for a steady grip just before he was taken on the volley.

'Of course the activities of X flight are quiet sensitive,' continued the Wing Co. with his introduction. 'So we shall be escorted with Warrant Officer Blaney for our little jaunt.' He pointed in the direction of Blaney, who was briefing a group of armed and camouflaged clothed troops outside the movements office.

'And who would be interested in the activities of X flight, Wing Commander?' asked Knowles, lowering his voice as he recognized a sensitive situation when he was in one.

The Wing Commander tapped his nose in a mock response, 'Let's not forget about our eastern neighbors old man.'

'Oh! The old iron curtain countries,' chirped up Knowles.

Miss Sally wasn't much up on politics but couldn't think for her life why anyone should use iron shades when cotton would suffice. The only benefit she could see for the use of iron was that it didn't need washing or ironing for that matter. Anyway, Knowles was the expert on geography and if he said they used iron curtains, then they used iron curtains.

'Yes, Mr. Knowles. A strong defense is what we need in this country and with the help of X flight we aim to keep it that way.' Wing Co. Flatly then slapped his hand off his thigh, 'Right, if we're all ready we'll be off.'

Miss Sally noted that somehow Warrant Officer Blaney's group had managed to disappear.

'No skateboards allowed, Mr. Knowles. You'll have to leave it behind sir,' said Flatly, glancing at Knowles old pal the Prince of Darkness.

'You're talking……. you're talking…..talking bout my feet,' stammered Knowles in disbelief. 'How dare you!'

Flatly rubbed his peepers with a hand before taking a second gawk. 'So they are sir. Goodness me…. you couldn't get a pair the same size I see. Gone for the asymmetric look, have we?'

Knowles managed to compose himself, 'They're not exactly the same size, Wing Commander. One contains a little more….what can I say….a little more power in it than the other,' said Knowles with a little bit of pride showing through as he slapped his hoof down with a loud wallop on the ground. June Daylo was one such person who could testify to Knowles statement. In fact, the inimitable flying machine that was young Daylo, just happened to catch Miss Sally's eye at that particular moment. The child seemed in fine fettle. Probably feels completely in her element what with all the flying paraphernalia around, thought Miss Sally, giving June a knowing smile.

Wing Commander Flatly turned in the direction of the group of pupils and clapped eyes on Primrose Green in the process. Quicker than a child licking a melting ice-cream, the Wing Commander whipped out a whistle from inside his tunic, put it to his lips then gave a shrill blow. An eruption of bodies appeared from behind trees, out of shadows, under stones, from anywhere, everywhere. One second there was nothing….the next a dozen men, all clutching guns had surrounded…..Primrose Green. Miss Sally knew that green children weren't the norm for sure but this was taking things a little too far.

'What's going on here?' demanded Miss Sally, to Wing Co. Flatly.

'Spotted a blighter in the midst of our group, Miss. All camouflaged out. Definitely an infiltrator to the establishment and all that hoo hah,' said a rather nervous Flatly. 'Warrant Officer Blaney seems to have the matter under control.'

'Don't be so stupid and all that hoo hah!' cried Miss Sally, pushing the Wing Commander aside in disgust before storming into the middle of the group of troops.

'What do you think you're doing?' asked Miss Sally to Warrant Officer Blaney who was directing the operation from inside the group of armed men. Blaney held up his hand to signal that he wanted the teacher to stop where she was.

'STAND STEADY, MISS. STAND STEADY. WE HAVE A HATA MARI IN OUR MIDST,' barked Blaney in his best parade ground bellow as he faced off the deadly Hata Mari.

'Don't you mean a Mata Hari?' enquired Miss Sally, referring to the exotic sounding lady spy from days long gone.

'Don't be fooled by the blighters changing their names, Miss. That's how spies work, you know.'

Meantime, Primrose felt quite bemused. She found the attention flattering but knew if things got to out of hand she could always rely of her newly acquired powers. Now what sounds could she conjure up …….. Something loud, foul, disgusting, or the good old painful and dangerous. Hmmmmm, she'd have to think it over.

'Now, are we being silly man or would you like to borrow my gleeks,' asked Miss Sally referring to her specks and Blaney's eyesight.

Blaney wore his peeked cap pulled so far over his eye line that he had an appearance of only possessing a nose and a mouth. The man was quite simply as blind as an Old English sheepdog in need of a trim. Blaney wasn't to be put off by Miss Sally's recommendation.

'Listen, Miss, there's been a few snurgle pusses seen outside the camp of late. We can't take any chances,' said Blaney, keeping his voice low without once taking his nose off his prey.

'What's a snurgle puss?'

'Female spy Miss. A Hati Mari,' said Blaney, his voice filled with venomous intent.

'Mata Hari,' Miss Sally corrected.

'Whatever, Miss. Just look at that camouflage. She looks like an overgrown flowerbed.'

Miss Sally felt like she was knocking her head against a wall. Warrant Officer Blaney had evidently walked into an iron curtain at some time in his military career and was still suffering from the after effects.

'That's how she is,' sighed Miss Sally.

Primrose continued to look down the two bore holes that were Warrant Officer Blaney's nostrils without uttering a word. The whole event was becoming ridiculous. Maybe if she threw her voice to emulate an attacking platoon of fellow snurgle pusses they might run off to leave her alone. She quickly dismissed the idea knowing that the trigger happy guards would be more likely to turn her into a human sieve. She sighed, hoping that Miss Sally could find a remedy to the situation before she was forced to take it into her own hands, which would only lead to even more trouble.

'Can't you get your men to lower their weapons Warrant Officer Blaney?'

Blaney took a sharp intake of air, 'I'll have to check her out first, Miss. The snurgle puss is a most devious creature, I'll have you know.' Blaney turned his nose from the Hati Mari snurgle puss for the first time since the confrontation to address his troops.

'If she tries anything, drop her, men.'

Very intelligent, thought Miss Sally. Considering they were enclosed by the circle she would be shot, Blaney would be shot and if they were really, really lucky, maybe Primrose. Yes, good move Warrant Officer Blaney. Good one. Blaney turned his nose back on Primrose and took a step in her direction.

'Don't move,' he barked, approaching the girl as if she was made of radioactive waste.

'Be my guest,' said a disinterested Primrose, speaking for the first time.

She was very tempted to give a loud boo, but the thought of being turned into a snurgle puss tea strainer returned. Blaney got within striking distance, reached out a hand then scraped his fingernail along the side of the girls face.

'Hey! That hurts,' howled Primrose, losing her sense of humor.

Blaney reached his fingernail up for closer inspection though the act looked more like he was about to pick his nose to the other observers, 'Hhhmmmm…..it didn't come off.'

He quickly turned to Primrose again,. 'Aha….one more test. This should give us a result.'

Primrose remained as cool as a cucumber, (well she was the same color), as Blaney extended his hand once more to……pull her hair.

'AGGGGHHHH STOP THAT.' was her painful response.
Blaney quickly released his grip on the girl's hair, 'I must apologize, Miss. We've got to be sure about these things you

know. A rotavator's what you need through that hedge.....I mean hair of yours.'

Miss Sally looked fit to explode. 'That's enough Blaney,' she cried. 'How would you like it if I stuck a pair of pliers up your nostrils and yanked your nasal hairs out one by one?'

Blaney's nose nearly leapt off his face at the thought of the torture, 'Not blooming likely,' he said, taking a step back from the irritated teacher. 'Dismissed men.'

Blaney and his cronies disappeared quicker than snow falling on an exploding volcano. One second they were there, the next nothing. Thin air.

'Are you ok, Primrose?' asked Miss Sally, concerned.

Primrose yawned, 'Just another experience Miss.'

'Good girl,' was Miss Sally's reply, before turning to Wing Co. Flatly who was in conversation with Knowles. 'Fat lot of good you two were.'

The Wing Commander was taken aback by the teacher's hostility, 'Can't overrule the security men, Miss Sally. W. O. Blaney does know his business.'

'The business of bullying you mean?' fired back Miss Sally on both barrels.

'Was that bullying Miss Sally? I thought the chaps were very civilized,' chirped up Knowles.

Compared to you they probably are, thought Miss Sally, but didn't say so. 'Why did they pick on Primrose?' She asked. 'We cater for all sorts in the services. Black, red, white....We just haven't come across anyone....well....green before. I think Warrant Officer Blaney was a little overzealous.'

Jemima Sally nearly swallowed her tongue. She wouldn't like to be around when the man got serious, 'Overzealous you call it?'

'You must admit, Miss Sally, that the girl is so authentic she could pass the fido test.'

Miss Sally was lost on the subject of Fido testing, 'Fido test?'

Wing Co. Flatly glanced around to make sure none of the children were within earshot then lowered his voice. 'You know the way a dog goes up to a tree then...'

'YES I DO, THANK YOU VERY MUCH,' interrupted Miss Sally loudly and in disgust at the Wing Co.'s stupidity.

Primrose, who could hear everything quite clearly, grimaced at the thought of the Fido test. She would tell them everything if they resorted to wetting her feet in this most despicable manner. Miss Sally's thoughts were along similar lines. Clearly the life of the real Mata Hari Snurgle Puss was wrought with danger from heavy iron curtains to affectionate dogs. Definitely not an occupation for the meek or unworldly.

'Is there any chance of you lot getting a move on?' said Knowles, tapping the Prince of Darkness impatiently.

Flatly slapped his thigh to show he was once more back in the saddle.

'Yes, of course. Now all that hoo ha is over, let's be getting on folks.'

With Wing Commander Flatly leading, Miss Sally fell in behind with her class, Knowles bringing up the rear with his. Most of the tour would turn out to be quite boring. Every now and again Miss Sally had to square her charges into shape, much as a mother hen chases around after her disobedient offspring. What the youngsters really wanted was the smell of high-octane jet fuel with the scream of a military fighter plane on song. The only excitement they had witnessed so far was the foolishness of W. O. Blaney with his group of snurgle puss hunters. At least, for now, they remained nowhere to be seen.

Eventually by way of the parade ground, guardroom, cook house, and doghouse, with a few other stopovers in between, the group found itself outside a huge hangar door marked by a large black painted X. The home of X flight's secret birds. Wing Co. Flatly faced the group of children who fought for space round the door.

'Alright people I'm going to hand you over to X flight now. I must stress....' Flatly's voice fell to a whisper, 'This is top secret.'

A hush fell over the ensemble. Top secret. Wow! Wing Co. Flatly fixed Primrose Green with a beady stare.

'All would-be snurgle pusses to be kept under control and all that hoo hah.'

Finishing his pep talk, Flatly rapped on the door with his knuckles. The creaking door opened slowly, adding to the air of mystery draped in secrecy. Inside a tall, dark figure stood in shadow. Rather than paying a visit to X flight, it felt more like an audience with the grim reaper. Atmosphere hung heavy in the air.

'Let me introduce you to Squadron Leader Wilson,' said Wing Co Flatly.

On cue Squadron Leader Wilson stepped out from the shadows. If ever a glance could say a thousand words then the one exchanged between Gavin Knowles and Toby Wilson was a telepathic version of the Oxford English Dictionary. Miss Sally caught the feeling of animosity immediately. In political terms this could be known as a tense moment. Squadron Leader Wilson meets Gavin Knowles meant nothing to Joe Public and Houdini meets the Prince of Darkness might have sounded like a horror movie to most, but to Miss Sally it invoked memories of the 48, (or 49), Schoolboys' Cup and she hadn't even been there.

'Toby Wilson!' cried Knowles as his right foot began its nervous tap.

Wilson's jaw went so slack it could have been mistaken for a pot holer's cavern,   'Gavin Knowles....what a surprise,' he said, struggling to find his bottom lip.

'I'm sure of that,' growled Knowles, not even attempting to cover up his anger.

'Oh, you two have met?' interrupted Miss Sally, waiting for World War Three to start at any moment.

'Played rugger once,' answered Wilson, offering Miss Sally a handshake.

'On the same side?' she enquired, already knowing the answer but trying to diffuse an explosive situation.

'No. Opposite teams,' replied Wilson, turning to Knowles to offer his hand.

Knowles gave an evil grin. 'Why not,' he said, lifting his own hand, spitting on it then offering it to his old enemy.

'Old rugby tricks die hard,' mouthed Toby Wilson, raising his eyebrows to show his refusal to accept Knowles' gesture of a free dose of tonsil bacterial minions.

Ughh! Filthy beast, thought Jemima Sally. The man must have been raised with a herd of camels. What manners, indeed.

'Now that you've all been introduced, I'll be off,' mumbled the Wing Co., chewing on his gobstopper, 'Enjoy your tour and all that hoo hah.'

Turning on his heel, the Wing Co strutted off, leaving Miss Sally with a rather large dollop of trouble to contend with.

Anyhow, Toby Houdini Wilson was nothing like Jemima Sally had imagined. Tall, slim, mustached, well groomed with dark hair, he seemed the perfect gentleman, but as everyone knows, appearances can sometimes be deceptive. Was there more to Toby Wilson than met the eye? Was he the creator of the twisted beast that was Gavin Knowles? The answers to these questions Miss Sally hoped to find.

With several other officers in tow, Wilson's security of the hangar was tight. Snurgle puss tight to be exact. Those children who carried bags allowed the Squadron Leader and his men to rummage through their particulars, not that they had anything special other than a candy bar or half-eaten sandwich to show. Since the children were being frisked before gaining admittance, so to was Gavin Knowles.

'What's in the bag Gavin,' asked Toby Wilson, spying the small sports bag that Knowles constantly lugged around with him.

Knowles' eye gave a nervous twitch, the edge of his mouth turning into an evil grimace. 'Oh, only a little friend of mine. A little friend of yours too, if you must know.'

Miss Sally, standing only a few feet away, nearly fainted. 'OH NO! DON'T! NOT THAT!' she felt like screaming, but the words wouldn't come out. She could only stand there like a helpless rabbit caught in the headlights of an advancing vehicle.

Toby Wilson seemed genuinely interested, 'Oh, let's be seeing what you have then.'

Knowles continued giving his evil grin as he slowly unzipped the bag.

'Don't look you'll be turned to stone, Houdini,' Miss Sally screamed inside her skull but still her lips remained closed.

Knowles pulled out another part of the jigsaw of the infamous cup of 48…or 49 vintage. The legendary….history making….Bertha.

'Recognize the little beauty, Toby?' asked Knowles, glancing from his beloved ball into the eyes of Houdini Wilson.

Toby Wilson wasn't in the least bit impressed.

'Seen one rugby ball seen them all.'

If Toby Wilson wasn't impressed, it was not the case for Jemima Sally. She stood transfixed as she witnessed the stuff of lore; legend becoming reality. Knowles rubbed a loving hand over the grotesque half moon shaped gouges on the ball's otherwise smooth skin. Miss Sally imagined Knowles probably reminisced of bygone days when he used to pick out the grime from his toes with a screwdriver or some other instrument from his vanity case. He wouldn't see those days again; neither would Bertha after her second hand manicure set had called it a day.

'Not just any ball, this is Bertha. She's one of a kind. Remember the 49- Cup? The old right hoofer? Up, up …… then out of the field.'

'Oh that Bertha!' cried Toby Wilson, his face looking like he had just seen a ghost. His eyes dropped to Knowles' right foot. 'How's your old hoof …. ,I mean foot, doing now?'

Knowles tapped the Prince of Darkness on the ground with a crack like thunder going off. 'Good. Bit of a customized job but I can still kick into touch.'

Wilson looked awkward, 'Yes, I can see you made a good recovery.'

Gavin Knowles didn't hear, his eyes took on a glazed look as he continued to rub Bertha's troubled, blistered battle scars.

'Myself and Bertha have stuck through good times and bad, the rough and the smooth. We were made for each other, Bertha and I.'

He then proceeded to lift Bertha to his mouth, planting a kiss on her smooth back. 'Weren't we, girl? Just you, me and the old right hoofer. The Trinity.'

Miss Sally thought aloud. 'So it was the 49 cup then?'

Knowles eyes snapped round to the slender framed teacher, the rugby balls narrowing to become slits.

'Do you think I would ever forget?'

'I assume not,' replied Miss Sally, casually, as she turned to Houdini Wilson.

'Are we getting on with this tour or not, Squadron Leader?'

Toby Wilson was relieved that Miss Sally had broken the spell of the dreaded 49-cup. Some things were best forgotten.

'Because of the size of this group,' began Toby Wilson, addressing the group of kids.   'I think it would be wiser to divide into two. Half will go with me, half with my 2ic.'

'Military term for second in command,' muttered Knowles to anyone who cared to be listening. Nobody was. He continued stroking Bertha affectionately.

'Right, who would like to join my group,' continued Squadron Leader Wilson taking a step back as he signaled with his hand for a line to form in front of him.

'I'll go,' Miss Sally said, without any hesitation. Her utmost thoughts were to keep the two antagonists apart, so to that end it was more sensible she partnered Toby Wilson.

'My class here,' shouted Miss Sally, trying to assemble her rabble into some kind of line.

When Squadron Leader Wilson was satisfied that all the kids were intact, he nodded to one of his men to close the door. Miss Sally was glad if nothing else that there was no sign of W.O. Blaney with his snurgle puss brigade. Now all that she had to contend with was World War Three. Staying close behind, Toby Wilson, Miss Sally and her class, set off down the humungous hangar for their tour. Left behind in the second group, Gavin Knowles seethed. It had been far too long since his last tussle with Houdini Wilson, so being separated was out of the question. Anyway, The Trinity was in town and wouldn't take no for an answer.

In the far distant section of the hangar, a speck of light filtered in as the giant doors parted to let in a returning X flight jet. Shining brightly, the aircraft taxied in to join the other row of secret birds. The roar from the jet engine had everyone clapping their hands over their ears. One person took no notice of the jet. Gavin Knowles never once took his eyes off the retreating form of Toby Houdini Wilson. When he judged the distance between them to be just perfect, his eyes threatened to bore a hole into the back of Wilson's head. Knowles was no longer in the X flight hangar; he had removed himself to a dark sinister place that was his subconscious. In his mind's eye he was back to the Schoolboy Cup final of 49, St Andrews against Black Friars. The roar of the advancing jet was the roar of an appreciative crowd. Knowles had already initiated the holy ritual of The Trinity but this time...,.yes, this time....he wouldn't be caught off-guard by a place kick.....he would use the volley.

The war cry of 'GERONIMO' filled the air, drowning out the roar of the jet. Bertha was in space as the giant anvil the Prince of Darkness sought to kiss her flanks. The two came together with perfect timing. A perfect volley. Bertha propelled down the hangar as if attached to an invisible string dancing inches above the heads of the children. If Bertha should get anywhere near Squadron Leader Wilson's coconut, or Miss Sally's for that matter, then Knowles would bag a prize. Only, this wasn't a fairground, things would look somehow messy with a head detached from a perfectly good neck.

With the reactions of a striking lioness, Primrose turned to roar at the missile, which was moving so fast it was a blur to the naked eye. Only Primrose's roar wasn't a roar…..out of her mouth came….silence. Not even a feeble croak. Nothing. It was not so in fact. Only to the human ear with its limited range of audio frequencies it would seem the girl was mouthing nothingness, however, Primrose had gone up several gears with her voice range into the high pitch zone known as ultrasonic. Bertha encountered the blast of sound as if meeting a solid object. She bounced off the invisible blow of pure energy, to ricochet several times off the side of the building, setting a new course straight for the incoming jet. The pilot's view, eyes that were trained for detecting an attacking foe, was not aware of old Bertha the rugby football but of a very dangerous man launched missile. With his base at present on a snurgle watch there was the real threat of some subterfuge plot to rumble X flight. His reaction was immediate upon seeing the blur of Bertha enter his jet intake. His finger touched the trigger of the ejector seat to catapult him up, up and away.

There was a loud 'WHOP....CRASH...TINKLE SCHREESH,' as Bertha tried the compressor blades of the jet engine for size. As the blades shredded like matchwood, the jet engine finally expired with a final feeble 'poop.' If the sound from the dying experimental aircraft wasn't enough to scare the living daylights out of everyone then the cry of 'SNURGLE ATTACK,' put everyone in the region of a cardiac attack.

'Oh no!' screamed Miss Sally, covering her eyes as the security team appeared from out of nowhere.

Smoke grenades were going off, bodies abseiled from the roof and men armed to the teeth appeared from every nook and cranny of the hangar to surround the X flight aircraft.

'WOW! They certainly know how to put on a show,' Bert Eccles guffawed, thinking the whole masquerade was put on for their benefit. 'Even the plane blowing up. It's so real.' Bert couldn't have been more wrong, though like nearly everyone there, he was unaware of who, or what, had caused the catastrophic demise of the X flight jet engine.

Among the general confusion of smoke mixed with the excited shouts of the school kids, Warrant Officer 'The Nose' Blaney and his team ringed the aircraft as if it were the crown jewels. So far no one had thought of the poor distressed pilot, whose only mistake was to forget there was a roof over his head, or that he was on the ground, when he punched out. Now he made like a cork in a bottle, still strapped to his ejector seat but now firmly jammed head and shoulders through the roof of the hangar where his cries for help went unaided.

Reeling from the impact of his actions, Gavin Knowles only thoughts were of Bertha. What had become of the dear old girl? Houdini Wilson had thwarted his plans once again. Instead of Wilson's coconut getting sucked into the jet pipe poor old Bertha had taken the leap in his place. Bonded together by blood and bone they were. The Trinity. A few armed guards couldn't stop Gavin Knowles from crossing the line to get to his beloved. If Blaney's team were there to repel a snurgle attack then they were about to meet the unexpected; The Trinity.....well two of The Trinity to be exact.
Knowles trademark 'GERONIMO' reverberated round the hangar as he began his headlong dash. Not since the Charge of the Light Brigade had such a reckless daring attack been launched. Knowles darted into the receding smoke like a tornado with a bad case of wind after demolishing a baked bean factory. In a flurry of arms, legs and bodies; he kicked, bit, butted and biffed the stuffing out of the security team. In a few scant seconds he had fought his way to the rear of the aircraft, leaving in his wake the guardians of X flight battered to a pulp,

not a single shot having been fired. Knowles suddenly wished he hadn't. There he found the metamorphosis of his once beautiful Bertha. Having not fared too well through the mincing machine that was the jet engine, she lay like a heap of stringy, dried spaghetti. The only way Bertha would team up again with Knowles and the Prince of Darkness would be in the reincarnation state as a pair of bootlaces. She was for want of a better word.....deceased. If Bertha was deceased, then Knowles was certainly the opposite. Mad as blazes, the dispatching of Blaney and his boys had only been a warm up for Knowles. His eyes bulged like bowling balls, his veins stood out on his neck like strands of wire, he was fit to explode. As his temper increased, he spied the cause of all his problems in the first place.....Toby Wilson. Knowles physically expanded in stature as blood flowed through his veins like lava from a volcano. He was about to venture forth on a Toby Wilson crusade. There was still some unfinished business between the two of them, bad blood that had to be put to rights. The ghost of the 49 cup had returned only this time the result would be different.

Squadron Leader Wilson, Miss Sally and the school children watched the entire proceedings as if in a dream. The kids were glad for a spot of adult entertainment which made their own pranks pale into insignificance beside this enormous cock up. Gavin Knowles was quite simply being a bad boy or, in mathematical terms, a bad boy squared. You couldn't get much badder than that, or so Miss Sally thought anyway. As Knowles stared the slim Squadron Leader down, Miss Sally was reminded of the biblical David facing the fearsome Goliath.

'Run, Houdini,' she felt like screaming, but she was caught in the car headlights once again, her jaws locked tight.

Primrose kept a close eye on the confrontation, waiting to pull another trick from her repertoire if so needed. The atmosphere was tense, the only sound the rhythmic tapping of the Prince of Darkness as he anticipated his next move. Miss Sally was sure Toby Wilson would bolt, but he too seemed transfixed unable to move, waiting for the inevitable. Death.

Then Toby Wilson did the strangest thing. Quite slowly, deliberately Squadron Leader Wilson aka Houdini Wilson aka David stepped forward to meet Gavin Knowles aka Dark Destroyer aka Prince of Darkness aka Goliath aka all round bad boy squared. A gasp escaped Miss Sally's lips as well as a few of the children's. She was certain Wilson's head would surely be torn from his shoulders. Perhaps Knowles would even stuff it into his sports bag to be brought out on special occasions to

remind him of the 49 cup. He might even give it to Chester
Smyth who could display it with his own trophies or as an
afterthought use it as a paperweight.

The two participants of the 49- cup sized each other up like two
prizefighters waiting to see who would make the first move.
Knowles wasn't about to lose out a second time and therefore
went on the offensive, closing down the distance between
himself and Toby Wilson. Toby Wilson remained steady as a
rock as Knowles got within spitting distance.
'Stop there! I've got something to say,' barked Wilson in an
authoritative tone that stopped Knowles in his tracks for a
fraction of a second.
Last words of a condemned man, thought Miss Sally, waiting
for the Squadron Leader about to take his last flight courtesy of
the old right hoofer. Ohhhhhhh!
'Too late. Your time's up, Wilson. You thought you had me at
the 49- cup, but as you should know better than anyone.....it's
never over until the right hoofer swings,'

Miss Sally wanted to close her eyes, but couldn't. The end was
going to be simply a violent bone crushing spectacle, all for the
memory of a rugby ball who once dared to become offspring of
Knowles due to a few sweaty old toenails from the old right

hoofer. Big deal. Waken up you moron, you should be praising Toby Wilson for bringing such joy into your life, instead of kicking him into touch. Forever.

'I assure you it had nothing to do with me,' said Wilson, remaining cool to the very end.

'Say your prayers. It's over.'

'One more thing. Just hear me out.'

The tension was mounting, the scene set. Everyone held their breath, daring not to move. Primrose was on red alert about to step in at any moment to save the life of Toby Wilson. Miss Sally was rooted to the spot, still caught in the car headlights. The only person who couldn't give a toot was the one on the receiving end. Toby Wilson.

Wilson's finger pointed upwards, 'Look up Gavin.'

'The oldest trick in the book,' sneered Knowles, pawing the ground with the old right hoofer. 'Look up and you get a kick in the shin. You must think I'm a complete idiot.'

Toby Wilson gave a knowledgeable smile, 'Please yourself then.'

To show that all conversation was at an end, Knowles slammed the Price of Darkness on the ground with such ferocity that he set off a minor tremor. Miss Sally blinked and in that moment....'CRASHHHHHHH.'

Jemima Sally half expected to see Toby Wilson spread all over the hangar floor, or at least about to be taken on the volley, but he was still there in mid smile. What had happened? The answer lay with Gavin Knowles, or to be more specific, the old right hoofer. One minute Knowles was standing upright, the next he was felled like an ox. If he had only heeded 'Houdini' Wilson's warning to look up at the hangar roof then he might have noticed that he was standing under the pilot who was still strapped to his ejector seat. The minor tremor he set up when he slammed the POD on the ground was enough to dislodge the pilot and the seat whose return to earth was nicely cushioned by the muscular teacher. Knowles hadn't even managed to utter the immortal 'Geronimo' before being sent into the land of slumber.

'Luckily the chute didn't open or he might have floated away,' said Miss Sally, quickly taking stock of the situation as Toby Wilson pulled the dazed pilot from his seat.

'Precisely,' was Wilson's reply, straightening up the pilot who clicked his heels together, saluted his senior officer and proceeded to keel over and faint

'Delayed shock I reckon. These young sorts nowadays aren't used to the rough and tumble of us old types. A little up and over never did anyone any harm.'

'I don't know about that, Squadron Leader. It doesn't seem to have done your friend any good either,' said Miss Sally, looking in the direction of Knowles.

'I did warn him,' sighed Wilson, 'but old Gavin was never one to take a warning, if you know what I mean?'

Houdini Wilson had played another perfect stroke in placing Knowles directly under the pilot. Miss Sally had the man marked as a master psychologist, adept at understanding human nature. By telling Knowles to look up, he knew the knuckle dancer would do exactly the opposite. If Knowles would have followed his old quotes regarding gravity he would have remembered, 'what goes up must come down.' BINGO! Goodnight Mr. Knowles. As Squadron Leader Wilson lifted the seat off Knowles, the children realized for the first time that maybe the bulletproof teacher wasn't going to walk away from this scrape. Face down on the concrete floor, with a bump the size of a pumpkin rising on his head, he was well out of the picture.

Everyone who had come in contact with Knowles over the years had memories of bullying, geography lessons into the next county, stretched ears and sore rears. Not anymore. With the ogre down and out, a roar escaped from the youngsters as they ran amok, using Knowles back as a springboard. The more adventurous of the children were already moving through the other comatose adults in their quest for souvenirs and goodies. Squadron Leader Wilson knew it was time to play his ace before things got too out of hand. 'Listen up folks,' he shouted, managing to attract some attention. 'There's going to be a free nosh up in the officers' mess. Soda pop, cakes, ice cream...all that sort of thing. Anyone who is interested should line up at the far end of the hangar now.'

The bait was fat, juicy and literally very edible. Drooling at the thought of food, the children were primed for a feast. Stowing away what goodies they could conceal, they started off down the hangar.

'What about all this mess?' enquired Miss Sally to the Squadron Leader, as she surveyed the destruction of both man and machine.

'I think we should start with an ambulance,' said Wilson, looking around for his own junior officers who only now were appearing from out of their hidey holes.

'Would someone ring me an ambulance?'

'Yes, sir,' shouted a young lieutenant, running off to get the nearest phone.

'You're right; it is a bit of a mess, Miss Sally. Gavin overreacted there. I think it's going to have to be a strait jacket and the nut house for him until he gets over the grieving period.'

'Grieving?' Miss Sally enquired, still trying to take in the enormity of Knowles moment of utter madness.

'Bertha,' replied the Squadron Leader in a respectable tone, reserved for the deceased.

'Oh!' said Miss Sally as things fell into place. 'Now that is something I would like to ask you about.'

'Fire,' said Wilson, walking down the hangar with Miss Sally beside him.

'It's about Bertha.'

'Yes?'

'Did you replace the original ball during the game?'

Toby Wilson fixed Miss Sally with a knowing look, 'Oh, come on now.'

'I would like to know. It seems so….well…'

'Devilish a trick?' interrupted Wilson.

'Well did you?' enquired Miss Sally, throwing all of her tactfulness to the four winds as she hoped to solve the riddle more fascinating than the building of the ancient pyramids.

'A magician never reveals his secrets.'

'Well did you do the switch?' persisted Miss Sally, keeping the momentum of the conversation geared toward a confession from Houdini.

'Yes,' replied Wilson in a casual fashion.

Miss Sally's mouth dropped. Though she was waiting for an answer she didn't quite expect Wilson to be so forthright in his confession. 'But what a terrible trick to deform another player like that. How could you ever dream up such a dirty lowdown trick?'

Wilson gave Miss Sally a smile, 'They were very attached those two.'

Such a cold-hearted attitude, thought Jemima Sally. 'Only when you placed old Bertha on the pitch for that awful kick. Terrible.'

'Spare me the superlatives, Miss Sally. The fact remains that Bertha and Knowles were very well acquainted even before the kick.'

'But you did the switch. You set the ball up for Knowles.'

Toby Wilson sighed, 'It might have been seen that way. That when the ball went out I did the switch.'

Miss Sally pointed her finger at the Squadron Leader. It seemed to her that on one side he was admitting his part, but on the other hand he was laying the blame, (literally), at another's feet, 'There you go. Another admission. How dastardly, sneaky, lowdown and cowardly a trick to play on anyone.'

Though Miss Sally was ranting on, she was in no way trying to stick up for Gavin Knowles, rather it was the principle of the despicable deed in the first instance and why anyone should go to those lengths in the name of sport.

Knowles dropped his head, his voice lowering, 'The thing that people aren't aware of was that I had no intention of doing the switch in the first place. Knowles bootlaces, fair enough.'

'You weren't going to do the switch then?'

'No.'

Miss Sally nearly believed him, though she knew he wasn't called Houdini for nothing. Was he just telling her what she wanted to hear?

'Where did Bertha come from then'?

Wilson scratched his head, as he tried to place the events of the 49-school boy cup.

'When we gave the penalty to St Andrews I booted the ball out of the pitch in frustration. Realizing it was a stupid thing to do, I ran after the ball. By chance the ball rolled over to Knowles' hold all which he always left by the side of the pitch during the match.' Wilson stopped talking as he pondered over what happened next.

'Ah! When I got to the bag I realized it had been knocked over by the contact with the ball, so upon moving the bag to get the ball, I now saw two balls.'

'Two,' said Miss Sally, trying to form a mental picture of the event.

'Yes, two.'

'What did you do then?'

'Well both looked the same to me. By that time the crowd was shouting, the ref. was blowing his whistle….I grabbed a ball, stuck it under my arm and headed back to the pitch.'

'Bertha,' gasped Miss Sally, her peepers growing ever wider. 'Didn't you notice any difference?'

'Sure enough, it felt a bit heavier but not unduly so. As you get more tired during the game, the ball always seems heavier.'

Miss Sally's eyes were wider than ever, 'So Bertha was Knowles' all along? Why didn't you tell anyone?'

Wilson sighed deeper than ever. 'Too late then, the deed was done. Knowles was hardly going to shop me now, was he?'

'My goodness but everyone thinks you did…'

'The dirty deed,' interrupted Wilson. 'It's only rumor. Knowles won't talk and certainly Bertha won't. He hoped to play her that day in that exact scenario, but to my team.'

'But he didn't get the chance and things backfired on him when you lifted the wrong ball?'

Wilson gave a smile. Sharing the secret of Bertha somehow eased the feeling of guilt he had carried round since the cup final. Miss Sally could hardly contain her excitement. Fact, reality, myth and rumor were no longer converging, but rather diverging. She now knew the truth, but what good was it? Who could she tell? It didn't matter. Some bones were best left buried and this one should be buried deeper than most. If Miss Sally thought only three people shared the secret of the 49-cup, then she had overlooked a little birdie. That little birdie was the elephant-eared Primrose Green.

Nearing the end of the hangar, the doors were already opening to reveal a line of ambulances. The eventful trip to X flight was nearly over; it just remained for the nosh up in the officers' mess. For once, Miss Sally could see why X flight wanted to keep its anonymity. All in all, as public relations go, the day had to be viewed in its entirety; a disaster.

Chapter 10

Squadron Leader Toby Wilson checked the remainder of Red Kep's young citizens before they boarded their buses. Suitably relieved of any knick-knacks such as grenades, guns or top-secret aircraft parts, he deemed the school kids clean to leave the military establishment. A final departing wave to Miss Sally, who was in the second bus, then the Squadron Leader set about his duties.

As he walked back to X flight's hangar the catastrophic events of the last few hours came flooding back as an ambulance, lights flashing, with a screaming siren, headed for the outside world. Not so for the ambulance's occupant, however. Trussed up in a strait jacket, tighter than a sardine in a tin, Gavin Knowles cussed as he swore revenge for his incarceration. A spell of counselling, proper medication, topped with liberal doses of electric shock treatment might eventually return Knowles to a status close to normality. Love affairs were always hard to recover from….even ones involving inanimate objects. Miss Sally was also thinking about the day's events, though now that she had met Houdini Wilson in the flesh, he was more a knight in shining armour rather than the rogue depicted in the 49 cup epic. Now Gavin Knowles was another kettle of fish entirely.

They were a few miles out from the air force base when Primrose had the first inkling that something strange was afoot. Above the mechanical humdrum of the bus' moving parts, she detected the faraway echo of nature. The thump of a cloven hoof on grass, laboured breathing of animals in motion…then there was another sound, something she couldn't quite figure out. Where Primrose sat on the left hand rear side of the bus, she was able to open a window to get a better understanding of what was going on. Fine-tuning her hearing, Primrose was able to dissect the manmade rhythms from those of a more natural occurrence. Hooves thudding on grass and stone, animals snorting as they sucked in much needed oxygen, the pounding of earth, then a strange unnatural 'gloorg.' The sound was similar to that of someone pulling their wellington boot from a slurpy mud hole. Primrose couldn't be absolutely sure, so she listened a little harder. The pounding increased as it drew ever closer…the laboured breathing, snorts, grinding…then 'GLOORG….GLOORG.' Primrose was no longer in doubt. It was Gibbs. As the realisation hit her, Primrose formed a picture. Gibbs was fleeing for his life. She didn't have to wait long as the fuzzy scene in her mind's eye became solid material.

Over the plain they came, a trail of red dust rising in their wake, a signature to their passage across the ground. The scene wasn't unlike that of a posse chasing an outlaw....Gibbs being the outlaw, while Miss Elle of the milk cow sisterhood was the posse leader. Once dinosaurs had ruled the planet, then it became the turn of the human species, Elle was now looking for her place in history. To Elle, evolution now decreed it to be the turn of the herbivores. She relished the idea of mobile vegetation; it added a bit more entertainment to the usual mundane practice of eating dandelions all day. Catching food fresh on the hoof was altogether more invigorating and healthy way to eat. It really worked up the appetite and got the old taste buds bouncing. For Elle and her girls this was the way to go. There would be no more Mrs Nice Cow.

Gibbs was starting to pay a price from the attack of the milk cow brigade. Like a pack of hungry hyenas, they snapped, worried, bit and butted the giant brussels sprout as he tried to stay ahead of their palatable intentions. The girls' delighted in the chase now and then biting off a tasty morsel of brussel leaf, just to remind them of how good the menu really was. It could be said that they were toying with their food. If Elle and the girls were enjoying themselves, then the opposite was true of Gibbs. It wouldn't take an expert on body language to see that Gibbs was in a stressful state. Too long in passing a diagnosis on the brussels sprout and the expert could forget about his opinion. Very soon Gibbs would be on his way to fertilizer land, courtesy of the Friesian milkmaid luncheon society. Not if Primrose Green was to have anything to do with it.

Though separated from Gibbs by a fence, which hemmed in the farmland, Primrose was sure that she could attract Gibbs attention as she formulated a plan. Her position from the rear left of the vehicle, closest to the fence, gave her a height advantage of any obstacles.

'Upty gloorgy upty dup dup,' she roared out of the window with all the finesse of a sea going oil tanker's foghorn. Though Gibbs' senses were scrambled, he reached out across the distance to find the shred of communication that spelt hope.

'Over here, get a move on,' was easier for Primrose to say under the circumstances. She wasn't the one having slices cut off her rump by a bunch of cannibals vying for the choicest pieces,

'We'll just turn up the heat for you? Like a magazine would you, Madame? Don't like your nose did you say? We'll have that. Ears a bit pointy? Two minutes and we'll lop them off for you. A sprig of cloves for your cold. Certainly!'

So, understanding Gibbs predicament, she was hardly surprised by the rather short 'GLOOGGG,' reply, which translated from his tone, meant…'Aaahhh!'

With hope, however faint, in sight, Gibbs set sail for the only friend he possessed in this despicable, horrible, insane, chase me, eat me, milk cow, cabbage, brussels sprout crunching world.

Miss Sally jumped from her seat at the first bellow from the foghorn. Being miles from the sea, she presumed it was some irate articulated truck driver trying to get past on the rather narrow roads. Glancing to the outside of the bus she could see no movement of any other vehicles. The road was clear. 'Imagination,' she thought, relaxing back into her seat. A flicker of movement on her left side, close by the fence, caught her attention just as the foghorn belted forth once more. Jemima Sally turned in the direction of movement as Gibbs drew level with the bus. 'HOLY JUMPING JELLY BEANS,' shouted Miss Sally, airborne from her seat at the sight of the giant brussel.

Miss Sally thought she was in shock, but one look into the green orbs of the brussel was enough to tell her who was the most afraid. Eyes are considered the gateway to the soul, and it was clear from looking into Gibbs' eyes that he was in a living hell, waiting to be devoured at any second.

Miss Sally's attention was drawn to the sound of thunder, which gradually manifested itself into motion as if the bus was travelling across ripples in the road. A minor earthquake she thought, but was given an answer a few seconds later with the arrival of the posse. Left behind by Gibbs' mad dash to catch up on the bus, the girls had been forced to up their pace. Miss Sally was reminded of a nature programme where a pride of lions had cornered a defenceless deer. They had swatted, pawed, bit and teased the poor creature until the eventual... Horrible....she couldn't bear to think about it. Mother Nature at her cruellest.

The cows chasing Gibbs were no longer the ordinary, domestic milkers. Malevolence showed in their evil grimaces and they grinded their teeth in anticipation of the kill. It wasn't so much the need for food, as the need to cause destruction. Elle Moo and the girls had found power. POWER! Jemima Sally could see that the cows had a presence, a possession if you want, and an intelligence that reeked of sickening, unadulterated evil. What would they do when they'd ripped the vegetable leaf from leaf? A reversal of the food chain, perhaps? Chase the stupid human beings around a field for sport, set up a high street delicatessen serving pate à la school brat or maybe the human equivalent of a mushy sushi. Heck, they might even set up a Friesian fashion shop serving up fine speckled leather overcoats with matching calf length boots made from only the softest freckle skinned kids. Perfect for those long winter walks through muddy pastures. Perhaps Elle would go the whole hog, or in her case the whole cow, and overthrow the government setting herself up as Primoonister in the process. Was Jemima Sally witnessing history in the making?

Miss Sally shook herself out of her daydream, but the daydream remained. There, right by her window, on the other side of a fence, was a huge green vegetable. The Gibbs spectacle hadn't gone unnoticed by Miss Sally's pupils who now had gathered on the left hand side of the bus to rally for the underdog.

'GO FOR IT!' and 'SHIFT IT, GREEN BOY' were some of the shouts of encouragement from the school kids.

Miss Sally was still trying to make some sense of the madness, but could not find a logical explanation, instead she too found herself roaring out the window.

'Can't you see that this is a private hire bus...you...you stupid cabbage! The town service comes along at 3 o'clock.'

As soon as she uttered the words, Miss Sally felt rather foolish. It wasn't the creature's fault that he was about to become main course and if he chose to wait around on another bus he was likely to be a much reduced fare. Reduced to the size of a postage stamp more like.

The teacher sensed the presence of Primrose Green, rather than saw her by her side.

'It's not a cabbage, Miss. It's a brussels sprout,' said Primrose in a matter of fact fashion.

Jemima Sally was in no mood to be reasoned with, besides Primrose had just let the cat out of the bag by stating the giant vegetable was in fact a brussel and not a cabbage as she herself thought. Was the Green child somehow connected to the event? Miss Sally turned to look down the bus to her other pupils.

'Can't you see that it's a brussels sprout and not a cabbage,' said Miss Sally in a rather stretched theatrical voice put on for the benefit of Primrose, 'that's probably why he's not listening to us.'

Finishing her public address Miss Sally fixed Primrose with her most stern look but being the easygoing, nice person that she was, the teacher found the mask difficult to wear.

'I take it that your friend, the brussel, is a he?' enquired Miss Sally, maintaining her authoritarian stand.

Primrose dropped her gaze as she tried to avoid confrontation with her teacher. She had the greatest respect for Miss Sally, but the complexity of the developing chain of events had caused her to keep some people in the dark for their own protection. Until now that was.

'His name is Gibbs,' said Primrose, a little subdued.

'He answers to the name of Gibbs,' called Miss Sally over her shoulder to the other pupils. Primrose was letting more details slip by the minute. She and the brussel were on first name terms no less.

As a chant of 'Gibbs' escaped from Red Kep's youngsters, Mr Sands the bus driver was tiring of the antics aboard his carriage. The chain of events was about to become a chain reaction, which was to spiral out of control. To Sand's mind, Miss Sally wasn't keeping her charges in check. Now with all the bodies toward the nearside of the vehicle the bus weight transfer was making the handling very difficult. Enough was enough; he would pull the bus over giving the young teacher a right verbal thrashing in the process. Sands glanced over his left shoulder to get Miss Sally's attention, but wished he hadn't.

Seeing the green object bobbing along beside his bus had an instantaneous effect on Sands. The driver's usually lank, greasy locks reared up from his head to give him the appearance of having a porcupine jockey in the saddle. In his case there was no need to apply logic to seek for an answer to the unknown phenomenon. He found his answer in the dark portals of his brain, reserved for survival of his breed. Handed down through the millennia, he was reverting to his instinct for survival, the fight or flight syndrome. In times of extreme danger, humans found they had to make decisions without conscious thought, prompted by their need to survive a life or death situation. It was a kind of automatic mode if you will. Sand's animal instincts hadn't been lost through the passage of time. Though buses hadn't even been thought of when man first faced danger from some extraordinary dangerous beast, Sands was about to apply his own special update to the fight or flight syndrome. With his right foot flat to the floor, Sands spun up the bus' tubes in a shower of rubber as he set forth to leave behind the green monster. To all intents and purposes Sands had just met the unknown, the stuff of nightmares, his own sacred version of the boogeyman.

As the bus careered round corners in the vein of a scalded cat, Gibbs fell behind due to the increase in pace. Primrose's mouth dropped open in despair.
'Can't you do something, Miss?' pleaded Primrose.
Miss Elle's gang weren't about to be denied their grazing rights. With a burst of speed, they shot forward for the final scene. Gibbs was on the edge of blowing a gasket, both from the pressure of the chase and with the rancid hot breath of the moo girls on his body. The vegetable was very slowly becoming a lightly boiled brussel. Miss Sally rose to the crisis immediately. If Sands wasn't stopped soon, then everyone was

likely to become part of a daisy chain. Miss Sally fancied daisies didn't look the same when viewed from the underside and six foot down.

Jemima Sally was flung from side to side as she struggled to take up a position close to the driver from hell. She just managed to catch the edge of his seat since Sands clung to his steering wheel like he wanted to yank it off.

'Hey! Slow down, man! Are you trying to break the land speed record?' shouted Miss Sally above the roar of the protesting engine.

Sands teeth chattered as if he were standing on a mountaintop in Siberia with his boxer shorts being used as an ice bucket.

'ALIENS! ALIENS!' he hollered.

'Don't be so stupid, man. Don't you know a brussels sprout when you see one?'

If Jemima Sally happened to see ten foot high brussels sprouts leaping around her plate, then her Sunday dinner would have been close to a riot. That a brussels sprouts had taken to wreaking revenge for the decimation of their species was bordering on the ridiculous. The previous one that Sands had encountered was drowned in a spattering of brown gravy and offered no resistance when provoked with his fork. Was mankind to pay the price for years of slaughtering young brussels picked in their prime? Was this the return of the killer brussels? Not for Sands. 'If the hand fits the glove' is the saying, and to Sands the monster trying to catch his bus fitted his idea of an extraterrestrial to the tee. An alien it was then.

Miss Sally was in half a mind to point out the greater danger from the herd of rampaging manic milkers, but in Sands' current state he couldn't care less if a cow jumped over the flaming moon. He was on a ledge above the abyss, standing on a ball bearing with one toe while trying to swat a troublesome bee with a bucketful of baby oil. In other words he didn't stand a chance. His ears were made of cloth.

Miss Sally grabbed her chance as the vehicle slowed cresting the lower slopes of Red Kep hill. Gibbs was now left far behind without a chance to catch his bus ride. Knowing that there was no smoke without fire, Miss Sally seized her opportunity as the bus slowed. Reaching across Sands, Miss Sally turned the ignition key and pulled it out. The fire, or more to the point, the engine, died. The vehicle groaned to a halt. If Jemima Sally thought she would have to fight the driver for the key, she couldn't have been more wrong. As Sands bolted in the direction of Red Kep with his pet porcupine, Miss Sally applied the bus' handbrake.

Miss Sally turned to face her students, 'It seems we're a bus driver light. So may I suggest we stretch our legs everyone.'

The youngsters jumped off the bus, full of chat concerning their encounter with the giant brussels sprout.

'Hey! Where'd you meet that guy?' Bert Eccles asked Primrose, as they stood by the roadside.

'What guy?' asked Primrose.

'That brussel dude?'

Miss Sally caught the essence of the conversation so thought it better to save Primrose's skin.

'No mention of any brussels sprouts to anyone outside of this party,' said Miss Sally, loud enough to ensure everyone heard, 'We don't want to be joining Mr Knowles in the funny farm, now. Do we?'

Though grumbles of discontent could be heard among the troops, Miss Sally was sure they would keep mum on the story, for a few days at least.

'Primrose, I would like a word with you in a moment,' said Miss Sally, noticing Primrose starting to drift away from her classmates.

Primrose gazed down the hill, trying to pinpoint the whereabouts of the 'brussel dude.' She gave her teacher a dismissive nod, 'Yes Miss.'

Meanwhile, though some distance behind, Gibbs was still in the throes of flight, desperate to escape the milk warriors. Coming across a low patch of ground, Gibbs found his path blocked by a large puddle. At the speed he was travelling, he had no time to adjust to the adverse conditions. Hitting the puddle hard, he was amazed to find himself bouncing skywards in the fashion of a flat stone skipping off the surface of a pond. Though his leaves were ragged from the attention of the Moo Moo girls he still managed to give a little flap. This was more than enough to carry him over the hurdle, the fence. His landing on the road was hard, but at least he was safe. Rolling along the road, with the chlorophyll slowing down in his veins, he looked forward to less stressful times.

Miss Sally observed farmer Dixon roll to a halt in his tractor. Being Miss Sally's landlord, the two were on very good terms. 'Something up Jemima?' said Dennis Dixon, walking over to her side of the road.
'Yes! I've just seen a ten foot high brussels sprout trying to board a bus while being chased by a bunch of rabid psycho milk cows,' said Miss Sally, tiring of the whole day as she sought to release some of the strain from her scrambled coconut.

'And I've just past a guy running down the road with a hedgehog on his head. Just another day in the country I'm afraid.'

A few of the pupils shot Miss Sally their best 'you shouldn't have said that' kind of a look, but the remarks of the teacher were lost on Dennis Dixon.

'So what's the real problem then?' asked Dennis.

'I just told you,' Miss Sally thought, but didn't say, 'We've lost our driver. The one with the spiky hairdo whom you just saw heading toward town.'

Dennis Dixon pulled his cap down, as a blast of wind threatened to pull it from his head. 'What got into him?'

'Pressures of work drove him round the bend, I guess.'

'It's good to see you're still able to crack a joke, Jemima.'

'You got to or you'd end up half mad,' said Miss Sally, sailing close to the edge once again, 'I think we're stuck here.'

'Not to worry,' began Dennis Dixon, 'I'll just unhitch my trailer load of turnips, and then I'll shoot into town and pick you up another driver from the depot.'

'Would you?' said Miss Sally, starting to brighten up.

'Sure.'

The farmer was as good as his word, already on his way to unhitch the trailer. After firing up his tractor, he set off toward Red Kep.

Primrose had picked up the vibes from Gibbs before he rolled into view on the long straight of road that led to the bottom of the hill.

'There's Gibbs!' called out Francesca Dewhurst, spotting the giant brussels sprout.

The other pupils, hearing her statement, peered down the hill and into the distance. From their vantage point, they had a panoramic view of the countryside, the grey of the road, the green of the countryside, the dusty red of the hill. It was a view that Gibbs would have appreciated. Not far behind him, on the other side of the fence, shadowing his every move the milkmaids crawled tiger style, as they waited for their opportunity. Just then, a car shot past Miss Sally's group on its way down the hill.

'Oh! My goodness!' exclaimed Miss Sally, catching a glimpse of the car's occupants.

Fester Arkwright, all buck teeth and jam jar bottomed glasses, hadn't in his wildest dreams expected country roads to be so badly signposted. Philomena, his wife, wasn't helping things by giving him wrong directions, as she read from a map that was upside down. As it was, they were more than twenty miles from their destination, a seaside town, when Fester encountered the gigantic brussels sprout. A few miles earlier, Fester had passed a sign that read 'PLANT CROSSING' but it was no preparation for meeting the giant vegetable. At the sight of Gibbs, Fester wrenched at the wheel, crashing through the fence separating the cows from the road. Gibbs wasn't so surprised, carrying on past the car on his merry way. If car drivers took to crashing into fences, then that was their business. It was a strange old world.

A few seconds passed before Fester or Philomena realised they had departed from the road. As steam escaped from their damaged radiator, it clung to the outside of the car as if they were in a greenhouse.

'Philomena, are you all right dear?'

Philomena extricated herself from the map that covered her head by ripping it to pieces. 'I told you not to take that turning,' Fester's eyes, accentuated due to the thickness of his magnified lenses, looked larger than footballs, 'Didn't you see it, dear?'

'See what, you fool? I was reading the blooming map!'

'That horrible, big thing bouncing along the road! You couldn't have missed it.'

'Well you did. You crashed through the fence.'

The car was suddenly heaved from side to side as the Arkwrights hung on to their seats. Philomena Arkwright's nose had a habit of glowing red when she was in a bad mood. Now it glowed redder than a neon beacon. She wasn't going to be battered, bruised or dented without knowing the cause of her trauma.

'Go on, Fester, see what's causing that rocking!'

Fester looked scared, for Fester was scared, 'I'm not going out there,' he replied.

Philomena's nose grew redder than a volcano, 'You got us into this, man! For all you know, we could be hanging over the edge of a cliff.'

All Fester could see was steam, nothing more, nothing less. Even the inside of the car was beginning to condensate with their breathing. The vehicle lurched again.

'If you don't do something, there'll be trouble, Fester.'

Fester wasn't sure where the greater danger lay. Was it outside the car, or inside? He took the only option open to him. Gingerly, for he wasn't up to winning any medals for bravery, he gently wound down his window. The large surface area that was Fester's glasses, steamed up. As Fester wiped away the moisture, he heard a crack, not unlike a circus ringmaster's whip. He felt a tentacle-like probe come through the window, followed by another crack. Fester's glasses were knocked from his nose. Fester struggled to find light, but without his glasses he was blinder than a bat. As he wound the window down further, the tentacle reached in again, to whip him round the face. Fester didn't know why, but his reaction was to sink his teeth into the tentacle, which turned out to be rather hairy tail. His auditory senses were still at a premium and an unholy sound rent the air. This was to be the forbearer of doom. In a few seconds, their olfactory senses, (snoring organ), would be tested to the limit. The lights went out for the Arkwrights in a second. It would be a day Fester or his wife would never forget. Ever. A real stinker.

Elle's gang found that the car, though through the fence, was still obstructing their passage to the road. Using a little bit of girl power, they managed to displace the vehicle to get better access. They had nearly finished when Betty, one of the younger wenches, was attacked from the rear flank. Under severe stress, Betty did as most girls do; she went to the little girls' room. A final shove had them back in the chase. Elle Moo Moo's gang were back for 'Return of the Killer Milkers 2.' As their hooves crashed onto the tarmac, Gibbs nearly jumped out of his leaves. He had just re-entered the food chain…..at the bottom.

The congregation at the top of the hill saw the scene unfold as a picture book. Primrose's eyes flitted nervously for a second, and then she made to open her mouth and unleash her weapon of destruction. A tug at her wrist made her gulp fresh air. Miss Sally was the cause.

'Don't, Primrose. Let's try something else.'

Primrose blinked her eyes in response to the words. Anything was worth a try, but she wouldn't let Gibbs go without a fight. If bringing her secret powers into the open meant blowing her cover, then she didn't give a hoot. A high-pitched scream, the low rumble of an earthquake, the roar of a lion; any number of things would put the cowgirls to flight. However, as Primrose was in the midst of her classmates, her secret would be no longer.

Miss Sally's brain was like a pinball machine, as ideas ricocheted around her cranium. The plan hit her with the subtlety of a sledgehammer. Her eyes came to rest on Farmer Dixon's trailer load of turnips. Perfect.

'Right everyone, line up here,' shouted Miss Sally, dirtying her hands as she lowered the rear door of the trailer.

'What's up Miss?' asked a slightly confused Samantha Bradley.

Miss Sally was already busying herself as she bullied her pupils into a line,

'What we need is a line from here to the top of the hill. Then, when a person picks up a turnip, they hand it to the next person in line like this.'

Jemima Sally shoved the turnip into Samantha's hands.

'Go on, pass it, girl! Don't worry about your lily whites.'

As the turnip now passed from hand to hand, Miss Sally shouted for another turnip to follow, then another, then another. She continued to race after the first turnip as it moved down the line.

'Come on, move that turnip!' shouted the teacher, willing on her pupils.

'When the turnip gets to the end of the queue that person moves back to be the first person at the trailer. Get it?' bawled the teacher, in contrast to her usually fine voice.

Gibbs was already in trouble as the Moo Moo's took him at the bottom of the hill in a pinscher movement. A flurry of brussel leaves scattered into the air as Gibbs faced death. The vegetable screamed loudly, 'GLOOOOORRRGHHHY.'

'What will I do, Miss?' asked Andy Archibald, last in line, feeling rather stupid as he held the turnip.

'Fire the bloomin' thing!' screamed Miss Sally, prompting the boy with a shove in his back. He responded by rolling the turnip down the hill, then running to take his place at the trailer.

Jemima Sally was in sergeant major mode running along the line of pupils as she monitored the progress of the turnips. 'FIRE! FIRE! FIRE!' she called out, as each turnip reached the end of the line.

The teacher couldn't keep pace with the turnip ammo, as they set off down the hill like misshapen bowling balls. Her pupils entered into the spirit of things with gusto, as they could see what their teacher had in mind. Gibbs was aware of the trickle of turnips, since the cowgirls were forced to release their grip on him. The trickle increased to become a stream, the stream to become a torrent.

Still, Miss Sally was looking for a bigger impact. Things were moving too slow for her liking. With an amendment to her master plan, she got the children to push the trailer around until the tailgate was facing down the hill. Gibbs was already in transit toward their position when Miss Sally declared war on the Moo Moo's by tipping up the trailer. An avalanche of turnips cascaded down the hill. As the road became a moving, heaving mass of bouncing turnips, the four-legged creatures went down like ten pin bowls. Legs, udders and tongues were all moved into unnatural positions, as the cows fell victim to the deadly barrage. Gibbs made his dash for freedom, avoiding his fellow vegetables by a series of small bumps and rolls, finally reaching the sanctuary of the school kids.

'At least the blighters can have something to eat,' said Miss Sally, with some relief in her voice.

Bert Eccles shook his fist in the air, victoriously. 'If they can manage to get up, Miss. Yee hah!'

As Gibbs moved around in their midst, the youngsters were in awe. Huge, green, though not at his best, the half-animal, half-vegetable had seen better days. T he kids were relaxed toward him, for Gibbs was on the shy side and more than a little scared. Primrose managed to pull the brussels sprout away from the others, 'Gibbs,' she said, introducing the green creature to Miss Sally.

'Gibbs, what an unusual name for a….a brussels sprout.'

Primrose smiled, 'A shortening of Great, Incredible, Big Brussels Sprout.'

'Rather a mouthful, Primrose. Gibbs seems quite perfect. Pleased to make your acquaintance, Gibbs.'

Gibbs' reply was some kind of gloorgy.

'Brussel speak,' explained Primrose.

'Looks a bit worse for wear, and that smell,' said Miss Sally, pinching her nose and noting Gibbs was a close relation to a bruised brussel found at the bottom of the basket. The one you usually threw out. Ragged, tatty, a little smelly, Gibbs had the air, (odour); of a vegetable past it's sell by date.

'Don't,' began a concerned Primrose, cutting her teacher off, 'I'll tell you about him later.'

Miss Sally's attention was drawn to the bellowing from the cowgirl fraternity as they tried to regain their hooves.

'I think you and your friend had better beat it, Primrose. There's going to be a lot of explaining to do when farmer Dixon gets back.'

'Oh, you're right, Miss Sally. What a mess.'

Miss Sally's finger pointed off in the direction of the countryside, 'I think your best plan is to stay off road, Primrose. I don't think it's wise for Gibbs to encounter anymore vehicles.'

Primrose was already on the move, 'Good idea, Miss. I'll get Gibbs to a safe spot. Thanks.'

'Don't thank me…thank all of them,' said Miss Sally, gesturing with her head in the direction of the other pupils. An almighty roar went up from the youngsters as Primrose moved off with Gibbs. She waved back vigorously, as they made their exit. Gibbs gave a few 'gloorgglysss' to add some moral support. Coming to the first gate, Primrose opened it, gave a final wave to Miss Sally and the others, and then moved into the countryside.

Miss Sally was left with a heck of a problem to contend with but out of the chaos she hoped she could use concealment, a smoke screen. It was time for another briefing of her troops. As it was, the roadway looked like a bomb had hit it, and they had not yet rescued the poor unfortunates who had crashed through the fence. As Miss Sally was putting together her plan, she heard the first scream of the ambulance siren, going full tilt for the bottom of the hill. There was nothing she, or anyone else, could do since a vegetable-cow cocktail separated them from alerting the ambulance driver. How he didn't see the obstruction in the middle of the road, she would never know. Perhaps it was the hollow in the middle of the road before the hill began to climb, or maybe the driver had been distracted by something? Anyway, since the ambulance driver was travelling at such speed, it was already too late. The resulting 'CRASH' had both turnip and the odd cowgirl thrown into the air, as if someone had just bounced a ripe tomato off a wall. Miss Sally quickly made her pupils turn away from the ghastly sight. Dog meat for the local kennels would be served with a liberal side helping of turnip for the next few weeks. Jemima Sally's day was just going from bad to worse.

Kale Knarsnock's nose twitched from the red dust which covered the inside of his shop, but even more so from the news he was receiving. The Norwegian had a nose for news. The news flowed in fast and furious from several members of the local populace who knew the deadline for the next day publication was that afternoon. Taking the different phone calls, Knarsnock's green eyes strained as he wrote the details down on a piece of brown paper in the poor light. He scribbled down the details as best he could, but things were always more difficult to take down over the phone. After speaking to the last witness he looked at the jumble of letters jotted down on the brown paper. Though his elbows smudged some of the pencil marks, he had most of the relevant details. Dick Turpin's son....rabid _attle....beasts... beat...two...fester....Elle Moo Moo gang...two tourists...bodies...pulp...rotten...bodies..from wreck. Knarsnock set off with the news details to set up his print at the rear of the shop. He happened to miss another call, which came from the local constabulary. They wanted Knarsnock to put in a piece warning local people of an escaped asylum patient who had kicked his way out of an ambulance and was on the run. The call was too late. They missed the deadline.

Knarsnock threw the typeset together in a blur of hand movements and rolled off a mock up sheet of the headlines to see how it looked. He would throw the story together later, when he could remember all the minute details from the phone calls. As the sheet rolled off the press, Knarsnock felt uneasy on his feet. The impact of the lettering made him feel like throwing up. He wondered what sort of society he was living in. It would never have happened in his day. People were sick, demented, deranged, the dregs of the human race. Biting his tongue as his stomach churned like an out of control washing machine, Knarsnock set off for an appointment with the lavatory. When the Red Kep Recorder hit the breakfast tables the following morning, there would be more than a few wallpaper designs enhanced by splurges of baked beans, cornflakes or fried eggs. Knarsnock dropped the page as he ran. The headlines came to rest face up on the dusty red floor and the black letters leapt out from the white background of the page.

'DICK TURPIN'S SON BATTLES ELLE MOO MOO GANG.'

'RABID BEASTS BEAT TWO TOURISTS TO A PULP.'

'FESTERING, ROTTEN BODIES PULLED FROM WRECK.'

Chapter 11

Miss Sally had so much on her plate that she would have needed a dustbin for her side orders. The big event of the year, the Red Kep flower and veg show, was that very day and things were already starting to simmer. As a new addition to the Red Kep community she would have to show a leg.

So far the village was full of strange faces, all due to the Miss Elle farce of course. The story had filtered through to the national newspapers, to the extent that the village was now overrun by journalists. They had converged from the big smokes, after the faint whisper in the wilderness had matured into a full-blown tornado. The return of the legendary Dick Turpin's son, (who would have been over 200 years old); to battle with a South American bandit was big news in any lingo. Journalists could sniff a story better than a great white after a pilchard that's just had an oil change. News that Mr. Sands had seen a huge alien, sifted through the net and since he had just taken up residence in the nut house, this story could not be confirmed. Miss Sally was managing to keep her charges under a silence curfew regarding Gibbs, but how long this would hold was anyone's guess. Gavin Knowles had done a bunk, that much was certain. The rear of the ambulance's doors bore testimony to the power of the old right hoofer. His following escape, through pools of cow bloodied, mushy turnip led only to more rumours that a bigfoot was on the loose somewhere in the hinterland. Further down the chain, the arrival of Tiger Dundee, the acclaimed big game hunter, fuelled stories of aliens, extra terrestrials, bigfoots and highwaymen.

Well in the background, the slaughtered innocents, the Arkwrights, had managed to disappear into oblivion due to sheer embarrassment. Though out of sight, they still had the essence of eau de cowpat to contend with. Needless to say, it would take some very vigorous scrubbing and many days in the water trough, to drop the physical reminder of their encounter with the Moo Moo gang. How long it would take to cleanse their minds of the whole unfortunate incident, was a matter for an expert head doctor.

Red Kep had become a variable melting pot of sorts. The village was more like a trek to the Klondike. A spare bed wasn't to be found anywhere. Caravans, tents, cardboard boxes, sleeping bags and humans littered the fields and side roads. Camera and radio crews trailed around, trying to waylay folk for interviews or pieces of hot gossip. Not since the invention of the high altitude barbecue burner, had Red Kep experienced such a carnival atmosphere of big game hunters, bloodthirsty amateur detectives or the good old general nosey parker.

Miss Sally bypassed Mr Green who was giving a bespectacled member of the press a good old ear bashing outside the village hall.

'Yes some strange things going on here, old chap. Would have been showing some of my own little darlings, except for the sproutnik. Now that was altogether another strange event.'

'SPROUTNIK!' said the journalist, peering over his glasses and twitching his nose at the mention of a new snippet of gossip. 'Just hold on 'til I get my pencil and pen,' he continued, rifling around in his coat pockets for the tools of his trade.

'The stew thickens,' thought Miss Sally, passing through the mass of bodies which led into the walled garden of the village hall.

As the weather was exceptionally fine, most of the show was being carried out in the walled garden of the village hall. Exhibits and stalls were strewn around and a melee of people congregated at their favourite interests.

Miss Sally spied an extension, not unlike the green hedgerow that bordered the garden. It was Primrose Green.

'Primrose, where's Gibbs?' asked Miss Sally, in a whisper, as she approached the girl.

'He's not too far away,' replied Primrose, in a glum manner.

'I did notice he's going a little bit off,' said Miss Sally, as tastefully as possible.

'It's just that he's not getting nourishment, not getting rooted if you know what I mean.'

'Yes I do,' replied Miss Sally, 'vegetables do go off after a while. By the way, I must ask you, where did you pick the critter up?'

Primrose glanced around to ensure that no one was in earshot, 'Well do you remember that storm I was telling you about?'

Miss Sally's eyes glistened, 'Yes. Do go on.'

Primrose gave Miss Sally a quick update on her story, this time explaining her first encounter with Gibbs.

'My goodness!' exclaimed Miss Sally. 'What an out of this world experience.'

Primrose's hair bristled as she replied, 'In more ways than one.'

Miss Sally slipped her arm through Primrose's as she led her off. 'The talk of UFO's and aliens is maybe not too far from the truth and then there's been the disappearance of the old right hoofer.'

'Good riddance to bad rubbish,' said Primrose.

Miss Sally raised an eyebrow, 'Let's get moving.'

Tiger Dundee was on the scent. He had been for the last couple of days and nights. The creature he was tracking was proving to be very evasive. Twice, once at dusk, then at dawn, he had caught a glimpse of the beast, but the sighting was little more than a fleeting shadow. Dundee wasn't unlike a bigfoot himself. Six foot eight inches tall, hands like shovels, with hair that bristled out from the neck of his lumberjack shirt like he was a burst sofa. He was gargantuan. A match for any creature, even a bigfoot. The dogs which accompanied him were as impressive as their master and they weren't to be denied their quarry. The bloodhounds would follow the beast through thicket, wind or rain, to please Dundee. The chase was on.

Dundee had already discovered huge grotesque shaped footprints on several occasions. Realising that the creature wore some kind of shoe covering, Dundee knew that he was dealing with an intelligent beast. The shoe prints looked almost manmade, but on a larger scale.

The combination of stories emerging about aliens, murdering renegades and the like were clouding Dundee's judgement. Maybe this was a relation of the bigfoot he had hunted in North America, but alas had never got a whiff at. It was all a puzzle.

It was on the morning of the third day when Dundee caught sight of the beast not far ahead darting into a wooded area. To Dundee's hounds the scent was like a concrete path in the air. As their master urged them on, they covered the ground in a few scant seconds, led by Washington, Dundee's favourite dog. The first sniff that Tiger had that something was out of the norm, was when a humanlike yell broke the air. This was promptly followed by snarling from the hounds. Dundee checked that his rifle was loaded, and entered the woods in search of the commotion. Seconds later, the snarling of the hounds was drowned by a roar which Tiger would later recollect sounded not unlike a 'GERONIMO!' There followed a blood curdling howl that tore through the shrubbery, reverberating around the neighbouring countryside.

Every hair on Dundee's body stood up, making him feel like a human pincushion. The fearless hunter was visited by a sight he thought he would never see. His faithful hound, Washington, tracking through the morning sky, his tongue hanging out so far it looked like he possessed two tails.

It would be the last Dundee would see of his old friend. They had tracked cougar, beaver, moose and bear to name but a few. Wily old Washington had never ever shown the slimmest shadow of fear; he would go through hell or high water in pursuit of game. No fear! Until now that was. Washington's unearthly yell was straight out of the bowels of hell. Had he met the devil himself, Tiger wondered not far off the truth. The hound dog was just another receiver of the legendary old right hoofer. Tiger followed the path of the animal until he was a speck in the distant sky. Unearthly! The howl hung in the air for what seemed an eternity. Washington's departure from the thicket would be talked over for many years to come. He would never be seen again. The natives would say that the howl of the frightened animal could still be heard on the wind on a blustery night, as Washington hunted for his earthly master.

As old Washington was in flight, his compatriots weren't far behind, though they stayed closer to the ground. Running from the undergrowth, they cowered behind their master.
'Go on pups, get in there!' prompted Dundee, but to no avail. The hounds wanted leadership; they would take up the rear. Seeing that the animals wouldn't budge, Dundee tentatively stepped forward. The first step was the hardest, but Tiger Dundee took solace in the fact that he was looking down the barrel of a gun. He hadn't come across a wild animal yet who came packing hardware. Yeah, he would show the blighter.

As he entered the woods, with the dogs following a safe distance behind, Dundee was aware of an eerie silence in the thicket. Not a sound. Had all the animals fled? The hunter was aware that if he didn't seize the initiative, he too might be joining old Washington on a sky tour. With his senses at an all time high, it was the nearest Tiger had come to the mystical beast in a lifetime of pursuit.

Coming to a clearing, he could make out the tell tale signs of a scuffle; dog fur, footprints, paw prints and something else he couldn't be sure of. Lowering his weapon, he stooped to pick up the remnants of canvas. The claw and tooth marks told him Washington had drawn first blood. Dundee wasn't to know the canvas was once a straight jacket. Clutching the piece of rag, Dundee's eyes widened in horror. He realised the beast he was up against had some form of intelligence, as it sought clothing with the intention of covering up its nakedness. A worthy adversary indeed, he thought, sniffing the rag and then the air.

Maybe it was the spirit of Washington, the blood thirst of the hunt, or any one of a dozen emotions that entered the hunter's head as he swore revenge. Not since he had fallen from his daddy's Land Rover while on safari as a two year old, had he felt such an adrenalin kick. Then he had come face to face with a man-eating tiger. Side stepping the rush of the frenzied beast, young Dundee jumped upon the tiger's neck and he buried his fangs in. Children normally sucked on a dummy as a comforter, but Dundee junior was in the habit of chewing on his teddy's throat to help him sleep. The tiger hollered in pain, managing to throw young Dundee into the air, just as the youngster loosened his grip for a second bite. Dundee senior saw his opportunity to get a shot from his rifle in. As the man-eater dropped dead, Dundee junior fell upon the cat for seconds. He gnawed at the animal, not unlike a rabid vampire. His father was cautious, as he pulled the demon child from the carcass of the big cat, fearing that he too would suffer a bite of the jugular. From that day Wilbert Dundee jnr. was confined to history. The Tiger was born.

Tiger was far from being the archetypal hunter; his primal instincts had taken over. As his eyes glazed over, the backwoodsman did the strangest thing. Throwing back his head and straightening his throat, he looked skyward and howled like a wolf.

'HHHOOOOOOWWWWHHHHHH'

The pack hounds joined the chorus, ready once more for the hunt. Not far ahead, the howling only sought to quicken the pace of a bruised, ripped, battered and tired Gavin Knowles, as he fled for his very life.

Miss Sally stayed close by Primrose's side while manoeuvring around the horticultural show's shrubbery and various products aimed at the green-fingered army. There was everything from quack remedies to restore your hair, to pongy potpourri for snoring organs.

'Where is he then?' whispered Miss Sally, referring to Gibbs.

'Over here,' replied Primrose, pulling Miss Sally through a hedge of thick conifers.

Miss Sally fell through the other side and came face to leaf with a rather putrid, festering Gibbs. The poor brussel was barely a few leaves short of being a compost heap.

'My, he has got a bit of a whiff,' said Miss Sally.

'To put it mildly,' replied Primrose.

'Why did you bring him here?' asked Miss Sally, wrinkling her nose to try to omit Gibbs' overpowering scent.

'I thought there may be something knocking around. You know, like the elixir of life for plants.'

'I don't think there's anything that would cover up that smell, aside from dropping him into a skunk convention, that is.

Gibbs gave a despairing 'gloorg' as he rolled his big eyes, above fleshy folds peeling from his body. The unfortunate beast was rotting from the inside out, as the ageing process sought to turn him into a squidgy, rotting compost heap.

'Primrose! Primrose!' a voice called from the other side of the curtain of trees.

'My father!' said Primrose, in response to Miss Sally's glance.

'Time to make ourselves scarce, dear. It wouldn't do if he bumped into old Gibbs here.'

Primrose gave Gibbs a reassuring 'gloorg' and bounded through the trees, nearly knocking her father over.

'Hi Dad,' said Primrose, raising an eyebrow at Alec Green.

Just then Miss Jemima Sally flew through the trees, as if it was the most normal thing in the world to do, nodded to old Green, and walked off. Green was no fool, he detected something was amiss; however, he would play his cards close to his chest since he didn't want to upset his daughter.

'What's going on?' he asked her, in a polite manner.

'Nothing Dad. We were just going around looking at the exhibits and got kind of lost,' replied Primrose, hoping her father didn't pick up on the pong.

'That's my girl now. You be sure to keep an eye out for any suspicious characters trying to pass my greens off as their own.'

'Yes,' said Primrose, following her father away towards the show proper.

Alec Green stopped in mid-step as his nose detected the slightest aroma of veg that was well past its sell by date. Remembering Primrose, he continued to walk, though he made a mental note that he would return to the spot later for an investigative poke. Something stank.

Dundee was hot on the heels of the man-beast. Studying the ground, foliage, natural shape of the land; the hunter knew he was following an intelligent adversary. Now they were out of the woods, the beast, (or Knowles to be more precise), was finding the flat landscape difficult to cover. The fugitive would spurt across any open space, find a hedgerow for cover and then make another dash to a safer position. So far he was keeping ahead of the pack.

Dundee was sure the beast would be his before the day was out, though he was slightly puzzled. By his reckoning, the monster wasn't looking for open space. No! The trek led the hunter to the conclusion that Washington's killer was doubling back toward Red Kep. The beast had an evil intelligence. What mayhem would the creature conjure up within the confines of the village was anyone's guess. Would there be a blood bath on the streets of the unsuspecting sleepy village? Dundee double-checked his rifle and upped his pace in pursuit of the wily animal. The hunter wasn't wrong. Knowles, tired, hungry, bloodied and bruised, was looking for sanctuary. The only place to go was Red Kep.

Alec Green looked around to satisfy himself that he had managed to lose his daughter. That wasn't too hard considering

Primrose had decided to head in the direction of home since she had forgotten to feed Pippa that morning. Green took only seconds to double back to the seclusion of the trees. He was on the prowl for answers. On the outside of the thick conifers, he sniffed the air not unlike one of Dundee's hound dogs. Yes! He was sure. Decomposing vegetation. Not any ordinary vegetation though. To his expert snout, the smell was unmistakably that of mouldy sprouts. Thirty years, buried in dirt up to his nostrils, told him that. Often when his own sprouts had gone bad he would freeze them to kill the smell, throw some fresh brussels over the top and sell them off as new. Yes! Behind the trees was a brussel graveyard. Glancing around to check that he wasn't being followed, Green stepped through the trees.

Meanwhile, on top of Red Kep hill, other pongy things were also coming to a head. A hungry bird, waiting for a worm to surface from its hole, was the only witness to the implosion of red, dusty earth. A few seconds later, a dirty red stained weasel of a figure, holding a spade, dug his way out of the large rabbit hole. It was the human mole, Knarsnock. Twitching his moustache and blinking his eyes, the little man got accustomed to the light. Once familiar with his surroundings, he threw his spade to the side and reached into the tunnel to pull out a rucksack. Later he would fit a trap door, camouflage it, and then bolt back the two miles to his print shop. For Knarsnock wasn't just a printer. That was just his sideline. The true face of Knarsnock was that talked about at the air force base. He was the Mata Hari snurgle puss, sneaky beaky, enemy within- albeit of the male form. He was a spy.

His razor sharp ears, which were always tuned for any snippets of information, picked up the faint sound of dogs barking. The ferret-like creature rummaged in his bag, pulled out a pair of binoculars, put them to his eyes and scanned the ground below. He picked up the small line of dogs, scurrying after the dirty figure of a man, as he headed southward toward Red Kep. Knarsnock tuned his glasses in for a better peek. The red ferret-like eyes jumped from the small head when he recognized the dirty face of Knowles glancing back at his pursuers. The schoolteacher's clothes were ripped to shreds and he was barely managing to keep up the pace. Like a frightened fox, he was looking for a spot to go to ground. 'My business not,' said Knarsnock to himself in English, though in his mother tongue he thought, 'fool.'

Knarsnock's mother tongue was neither English nor Norwegian, though he spoke both in a somewhat mongrel manner. No, Mr Knarsnock was in fact Colonel Igor Popov of the notorious GKB. Nobody was exactly sure what GKB stood for, as was the case for most abbreviations, but the organization was made up of the most lying, cheating, thieving bunch of lowlifes assembled in the name of snurgle duggery. The Russian's cover of local rag printer was ideal for gleaning information to send back to his spymasters. For many years he had kept up the pretence of being Norwegian as he spied on the local airbase with its experimental jet aircraft. He was Popov aka Knarsnock aka Hata Mari, puss snurgle, sneaky beaky. Knarsnock turned away from Knowles' figure, set his binoculars down and reached into his bag to extract a camera with a super duper xxxx telescopic lens. It had taken him years to dig out the two miles of tunnel and he was now in the exact location where the X flights overflew on their training sorties. Perfect. He settled down for the wait.

When Alec Green burst through the conifers, he was greeted by both his greatest dream and as his worst nightmare. What he thought was a compost heap, moved when he touched it, to reveal the form of a huge, mobile brussels sprout. In the shade of the trees, he could even make out huge eyes and a leafy mouth. His tiny, pea brain went into overload, as he tried to take in the enormity of it all. All those years of crop spraying had come back to haunt him? Revenge of the killer brussels, but worse than that, much worse than that, was the stench! Oh the stench! Gibbs rolled toward Alec, perhaps seeing in him the father figure who had nurtured him as a seedling. 'Glooorghyy, up gloorghy,' said Gibbs, by way of a greeting. Alec Green's lip quivered like a fish on a pole. The huge eyes and the moving mouth took the dream into the realms of nightmare. Green thought he was about to be devoured by this awful, stinking monster. In his terrified state, Green did as he would do in a nightmare. Screamed! However, the scream didn't last long, since Alec Greens' heel caught a tree root, pitching him backwards to knock his head against a tree trunk. Now he really was in dreamland. The scream also had an effect on Gibbs, for he sought to distance himself from the scene. Though he had manoeuvred himself into the walled garden the night before by the brussel jump, he now took the hastier route of bulldozing a path through the conifers. With a bang, creak and rustle, he decimated a path through the trees to get free. Or was he free? No! Gibbs was still trapped within the walled garden.

Jemima Sally bumped into the Squadron Leader as he negotiated the various exhibits.

'How's it going, Squadron Leader,' asked Miss Sally, her face giving way to a hint of a blush.

'Fine,' replied Toby Wilson. 'It's nice to see a friendly face around here,' he said, smiling. 'Especially after all that trouble.'

'Ghastly,' said Miss Sally, though she knew more than most.

'So what's your view on the whole thing, Miss Sally?' the Squadron Leader ventured.

'Oh, do call me Jemima,' came back the smiling reply.

'Of course, Jemima,' said Toby Wilson, feeling more at ease.

Miss Sally steered the Squadron Leader through the crowds in the direction of Granny Knot's juicy, fruity jam stall.

She lowered her voice, 'Lots of strange things go on round here, Squadron Leader. The villagers are a very tight bunch and I'm an outsider.'

'Yes, I know what you mean,' cut in Toby Wilson, lifting one of Granny Knots fabled mixtures. 'Rhubarb! Mmmm, sounds too good to be true.'

Miss Sally did likewise picking up a deliciously colored jar.

'Not bad on the price either by the look of things, Squadron Leader.'

'Toby, if you don't mind,' said Wilson, glancing over the top of his jar at Jemima Sally.

'Sure, Toby,' replied Miss Sally, sheepishly.

Granny Knot observed the ritual sampling of her wares. She was a woman who could read a situation, and in this instance she knew the young couple had more than jam on their minds. Cupid was doing aerobatics round the couple before he found the right moment to set loose his arrow. When would he take the shot?

Gibbs broke cover to the rear of the garden fête. Luckily for the brussel, there were no pedestrians in the vicinity. From his position, he had an unobstructed view down the aisles between vendors, showmen, exhibits and prospectors. Gibbs stance was that like that of someone in the rear seats of the cinema. He could see everything in front of him, and as yet nobody could see him. Searching for a friendly face, the only person he recognised was Miss Sally who was talking to a tall athletic man in uniform. Looking to and fro, he could see no sign of Primrose? What would he do?

Knowles vaulted the wall of the garden like the frightened animal he had become, as he sought a place where he could lay up for a rest. Dirty, cold, tired, he needed a chance to recharge his batteries. A chance to think straight. Why had it come to this? Only a few days ago he was with his friend, Bertha. The world was his goalpost. All was well......well, until he bumped into old Houdini Wilson, that was. Through the grey areas of his brain, the memories of the 49-cup flooded back, served up with a bucketful of agony. Wilson was his conscience, his jinx, his Achilles, tapping away in the deepest part of his brain like some pneumatic drill until... Knowles wiped away the dirt from his face, while trying to control his inner rage, but his tired eyes only caused him more disbelief. Shaking his head, he closed his eyes, and then reopened them. NO! This was no mirage. No tell tale image of tiredness. No trick of the mind. No, this was something else. There, not too far in front of Knowles, was the real jack dandy, in the flesh, give me a cloven hoof please, Mr Big Shot 'I can do anything better than anybody else', super hero of the 49 cup....the one and only, Toby Houdini Wilson. Knowles' bloodshot eyes became a road map, as the red lines strained to explode from his peepers. It didn't help matters to see Toby with his sidekick teacher friend. The little trollop was another thorn in Knowles' side. Just then, a shadow crossed in front of the madman's sights and temporarily blocked his view. Knowles wasn't to know the shadow was in fact the rear end of Gibbs. To the warped mind of the demented teacher all he could see was a huge ten-foot high, smelly ball like shape directly in the path of....

In a split second Knowles was working out triangulations, trajectories, and speed equations for something of the huge target area. His ears picked up the first yelps of the hounds as they tried to scale the walls of the closed garden. Their sounds only helped him reach a decision. In the blink of an eye he was committed. Do or die. The spirit of the 49-cup revisited. In that moment, Knowles was madder than a March hair with a severe case of dandruff. He let out his famous war cry as he covered the few feet towards Gibbs' back end,

'GERONIMOOWWWWWWWW!'

The prince of darkness sunk deep into the fleshy regions of Gibbs.

The howl was like an air raid warning to the Squadron Leader. His trained reflexes had Toby Wilson throwing Miss Sally to the ground. Meanwhile, the right hoofer sunk deeper into the rotten mush that was Gibbs carcass. The surprise on Gavin Knowles' face lasted only a microsecond. Whether it was his forward momentum, a slip on a stone, a spark from the prince of darkness, whatever, it was just enough for ignition. Somehow a spark managed to light up Gibbs gaseous interior.

The giant brussels sprout took off like a bolt of greased lightning, leaving a plume of orange flame in his wake. Bodies dived for cover as Gibbs roared toward Granny Knot's stall of fruity preserves. The Reverend Jasper's jelly belly managed to save his life as he was thrown at a wall by the blast. Instead of being spattered like an overripe raspberry, he bounced off in the opposite direction like a basketball off a backboard. Those who said being overweight can kill had obviously never seen old jelly belly in action.

Gibbs' face was one of utter horror, while his body was a hurtling green meteorite, completely beyond his control. Granny Knot grasped her pram to put some protection between her and the missile, but to no avail. The pram bore full impact, absorbing into Gibbs' body on Knowles' planned trajectory, or was it planned? Knowles hadn't reckoned on Gibbs' independent fuel source. Gibbs wasn't about to stop as he now headed skyward with Granny Knot on the roller coaster of a ride. Granny Knot's usually wrinkled expression, became even more so, as she started to resemble an anxious prune that had been locked up in a Turkish bath at full heat. Meanwhile, the residents at the event were scattered by the blast like leaves in a hurricane. The extravaganza had finally become an exploding event.

Though heading skyward, Granny Knot had managed to catch her stocking elastic on her stall, causing some resistance to her heavenly flight. She clung onto her pram handle as the pram remained embedded in the brussel's body. She was in the dark as to what was really going on, since the pram obstructed her view. Going backwards in flight meant all she could see was a jade green, luminous, blinking light which was, in fact, one of the brussel's eyes. The only sound she could hear was the rush of air, drowned out by the roar of a jet coming from somewhere behind the green projectile. Straining her head to look downwards, she saw they had now departed the village and were heading over Red Kep hill.

Igor the red, snapped round with his camera, half expecting to see one of the super duper X flight aircraft. His focused eye leapt from its socket like a dog on a leash, at the sight of a huge brussels sprout being piloted by Granny Knot.

Furiously, he jabbed away at the shutter to capture the moment on film. At that very second, the outbound aircraft from X flight was also on its path above Red Kep hill. As the green missile filled the pilot's view, he slewed the aircraft to the side. This was enough to avoid a collision but somehow he managed to cut through Mrs Knot's stretched stocking with the tip of his wing. It was the final thread that separated the twosome from even greater heights to explore. Now with nothing to hold him to Mother Earth, Gibbs reached full velocity, racing up into the midday sky. Granny Knot held on to her shuttle vehicle for dear life, as she reached maximum G. Meanwhile, the wrinkles on the elderly lady's face bunched up, not unlike an intricate origami piece. In the blink of an eye the duo were out of sight.

'Jacks Holy Jumping!' exclaimed Knarsnock, laying down his camera. He had seen no less than a manned vegetable taking off into space! X flight had to have been a cover all along. Knarsnock, aka Popov's, brain clicked away as he assimilated the data. His face frowned, as he thought back to the high altitude barbie......farm combustion. Perfect fuel! Methane! X flight was just a smoke screen. The people in the village were the true rocketers. Why, he had just seen Major Knot of the sally army atop a missile, a huge brussels sprout. It was most likely part of the sproutnik operation. And the main operator behind that business was Alec Green. Little wonder he had thrown a wobbly when he had been robbed of his precious little sprouts. Knarsnock packed away his spy bag, readying himself for a trip back to the lair.

For those left behind, there were far more questions than answers. There were two famous sayings…'there is an equal and opposite force' and 'this will hurt me far more than it will you.' These statements proved to be quite right. Knowles' kick resulted in an equal force that blew him square into the next county. One of his exponents of the old right hoofer, June

Daylo, was out riding her bike when she saw the near naked, blackened figure flying backwards with all the serenity of a gob of spit. She coined the phrase 'a legend in his own underpants.' In fact, Miss Daylo was the last person in Red Kep to see Knowles' speedy exodus.

Thereafter, Knowles would never be heard of again, though stories would filter through over the years of sightings of a wild man beast living off the land in the desolation of the Scottish highlands. Many people presumed it to be another myth of Loch Ness proportions to bolster the tourist business, though others weren't so sure. Every now and then, a strange footprint or two would turn up on soft ground to re-kindle the story of the bigfoot. A flock of people would then descend on the site, the first usually being Tiger Dundee who still craved revenge for the demise of old Washington. Alas these expeditions proved nothing, as the beast remained as elusive as ever. If there ever was a beast. Why no one ever made the connection between Knowles and the bigfoot, was a matter for the scientific brotherhood, who had managed to cock things up once before by linking the teacher to a million year old Ethiopian chick called Martha. All that the Red Kep citizens knew was that if Knowles set the right hoofer on their soil again he would resume his career in the local nut house.

Meanwhile, Miss Sally struggled to her feet, helped by Squadron Leader Houdini Wilson. Others were doing likewise as they tried to make some sense of the madness. The scene was one of some destruction. There were overturned stalls, shattered pots, plants, earth, flowers, and vegetables all littering the ground. Every now and then, the carpeted mess moved and another bedraggled human emerged from beneath, glad to be intact.

Amid the chaos, Miss Sally spotted the green bush that was Primrose Green's head, moving among the shocked crowd. The schoolteacher knew that Primrose's super sensitive hearing would have already warned her that something was amiss.
'Gibbs,' was the only word Primrose used as she drew level with Jemima Sally.
'Afraid so,' replied Miss Sally, careful that the Squadron Leader wouldn't hear, but there was no need to worry since he was busy helping others around the blast sight.
Primrose shed a tear, but Miss Sally, ever the optimist, jumped to her aid.
'He was starting to decay, dear. It was for the best. Gavin Knowles had something to do with it....Then there was poor Granny Knot...'

Miss Sally was cut short in mid-sentence as more trouble arrived; Tiger Dundee's animals were frantic to find their invisible foe. Miss Sally glanced skywards, wishing for an end to a terrible day.

Back at Knarsnock's lair, the ferret-like creature was busy. As a plan formed in his head he continued his journalistic capers, running up a headline on his press. He watched the black ink capitals dry, satisfied that he had captured the essence of the first manned or womaned space trip.

'GASSING MAJOR, GRANNY KNOT, BLASTS SPROUTNIK 1 INTO ORBIT, HELPED BY ELASTIC BLOOMERS.'

'Mmmm, too bad not,' he mused.

Another part of Knarsnock's complicated plan suddenly clicked into place with the arrival of Alec Green banging at the newspaper man's door. The trap was sprung. Knarsnock assisted Alec Green into his gloomy, dusty, red, earthy colored parlour.

'It looks a bit like Mars in here,' said the farmer, wiping away a layer of red dust from a table top with his fingers.

Knarsnock's cat eyes narrowed at the remark. Had Green already launched a trip to the outer planets of the solar system? If so, then the Granny Knot episode was just one of a sequence of ongoing space expeditions. The flying children of Red Kep were not the result of a sadistic, overzealous twerp, but more likely part of some secret young test pilot school, geared for space travel. Things were becoming clearer to Knarsnock by the second. He knew that he would have to work quickly to secure his prize.

'Did you see it? The huge vegetable...my sprout,' continued Green. 'Did you see what happened? I kind of missed the finale.'

Knarsnock saw his chance, pushing Green into a comfortable chair.

'Perhaps special tea a cup of?' said the printer, his eyes starting to glow.

'Of course,' replied Green, 'in a clean cup please. One sugar.'

Knarsnock lifted the boiling kettle from his stove and poured tea into two cups. Green failed to see Knarsnock administer a shot of his secret sleeping juice into the farmers' cup in place of the sugar.

'Down you'll get it and I'll you'll tell what happened,' said Knarsnock, handing over the cup.

Within minutes, Alec Green was starting to doze off. Knarsnock's sing song voice, his hypnotic cat eyes and the heavily scented tea, all added to his feeling of relaxation.

Green's eyelids felt like they had been tied to lead weights. He slumped over, dropping his cup to the floor so that it shattered into a hundred pieces. Knarsnock smiled, looking like a cat that's just got the cream. Now his plans would go into full swing. That evening he would make his way to the coast, steal a boat, load the unconscious farmer aboard and set sail to rendezvous with a submarine. Thereafter, he would be changing his curtains from cotton back to iron once more.

In a year or so we would hear of a modified sproutnik, known by the Russian name Sputnik, this being an unmanned satellite. A further three and a half years would pass before the Russians would follow Granny Knot into space with their suitably named Cosmonaut. The date was the 12th April 1961 and the man, Yuri Gagarin. A world first? Few people would ever know of the first true space flight because the powers that be swore the people of Red Kep to secrecy. The sproutnik, Gibbs, Granny Knot partnership was to be forgotten in the name of embarrassment, common sense and national security.

Knarsnock's final headline would lie undisturbed for twenty years until property developers decided to bulldoze his derelict shop. Then it was used to light a bonfire with the rest of the rubbish.

Post-sproutnik Red Kep wasn't all doom and gloom. Children returned to school in a happier climate, knowing that they weren't about to be dropkicked for failing a question on local history. Primrose Green and her brother would no longer be a victim of their strange color. With a balanced diet, their color changed to something close to normal, though they still tended to glow, if only a little, in low light conditions. Primrose's mother was released from her life of slavery to a horrible master while he, on the other hand, was firmly encircled behind an iron curtain.

The story didn't end there for Primrose, however. Miss Sally saw in the girl a wondrous talent as an entertainer. With Miss Sally's coaching, Primrose would leave school to go on to be a successful opera and pop singer known worldwide. She would perform to sell out concerts and would duet with some of singings greats; Pelvis Resley, Britney Houston and Whitney Spears, to name but a few. Miss Sally's own wish was granted when she traded her name in for Mrs Houdini Wilson. She felt even better when Primrose made her into her personal manager. In their hectic schedule travelling the globe, Red Kep often seemed like a fleeting, fading memory. That was until Primrose thought of her friend, Gibbs, to whom she owed everything. Then she would have only happy thoughts…the wind rustling in the trees….a raindrop…. She found herself accelerated back in time, to once again stand in that field where the air felt electrified before the impending thunderstorm. Gibbs was only a few thunderclaps away. Primrose breathed contentedly, at peace…